# Additional Titles by

*City Steam Collection (Tempest Press)*
The Alchemist's Perfect Instrument (September, 2011)
The Krie Seekers (March, 2013)

*Hill Dwellers (Tempest Press)*
For Your Heart (October, 2013)

*Tricksters Series (Entangled Teen)*
NEXIS (December, 2015
REDUX (December, 2016)

# M.I.A.

A novel by

# A.L. DAVROE

Dee,

Stay Safe ....

*[signature]*

Tempest Press

Edited by Ink It Out Editing Services
Cover Design by CoverQuill
Interior design by A.L. Davroe

for those who are lost
and never found
and
for those who know where they are
but can't get free

you are not alone

# M.I.A.

# One:
# Corey

Cutter comes home at half past seven—which is later than usual. As his pick-up rumbles over the overgrown, pot-holed driveway, I make my way down the stairs and wait for him in the kitchen. He comes in whistling to himself and looking the same as always—beat-up work boots, dusty jeans, worn leather jacket, lanky hair tucked under a sweat-stained 49ers hat.

As he turns to put a six-pack of beer on the counter, I peak into the brown grocery bag he left on the chrome-rimmed kitchen table. "What did you bring me? Any snacks?"

Investigation proves that there is nothing for me in the bag.

With a pout I step back, letting him drag the bag off of the table and onto the counter. He begins stacking cans of refried beans and tuna in the mostly empty cabinet—*clack, clack, clack.*

Sulking, I lean against the counter and stare at the cracked floor tiles. "You never bring me anything," I mutter. "You don't think of me when you're out, do you?"

He doesn't answer. I don't expect him to. Cutter never answers. And I'm not sure he *ever* thinks of me...even when he's home.

Wanting to get his attention, I saunter over to the six-pack and give it a little push. A glance over the shoulder proves I've got it. "Oh," I say, annoyed that a six-pack is more important to him than I am, "you're listening now, aren't you?" With all my might, I shove the bottles off of the counter and onto the floor, shattering all but two which roll across the floor and clank into the stove.

"Jesus fuck!" Cutter screams, practically jumping onto the counter—as if I were a mouse and getting higher than me would do anything.

Delilah starts up barking.

A moment later, Cutter comes to his senses and, scowling, lowers his feet and stomps over to the basement door. He yanks it open and bellows at the hound below. "Shut the hell up!"

Delilah yelps like she's been kicked in the ribs, abruptly going silent.

Cutter turns back to the kitchen, closing the door with his weight. "Pain in the ass mutt." His eyes trail across the floor, taking in the frothing puddle of beer, then back to where I'm standing.

I try to look innocent, although I can't help my Cheshire Cat grin. "Oh come on, Cutter, you and I both know that drinking doesn't do anything to improve your mood."

Still leaning against the basement door, he rubs at his eyes. "God damned nuts."

"Nuts?" I reply. "Good idea, I'd love to know what you did with mine."

Cutter turns his back on me and gropes for one of the undamaged beer bottles. He shakes the condensation off of it and snaps it open on the edge of the counter. "Just gotta get back into yourself," he's saying.

"I doubt I'd like what I found."

He turns and walks away from me. "...gotta feel alive again."

There's no hope of that. But I don't think he's talking to me. Frowning to myself, I follow him. "And just what does that mean?"

He stops inside the dimly-lit hall, his bloodshot brown eyes caressing a closet door. Uncertain, I stare with him as he continues mumbling to himself. "...gotta make your mark on the world. Gotta show them who's in charge." He takes a swig, his eyes never leaving the paint-cracked door.

I cross my arms. "You're *insane*. Has anyone ever told you that?"

His hand comes up, tugs the 49ers cap backward and traces fingers through thin mud-colored hair, then he puts the cap back on and nods once. "Yeah. 'Bout time, old friend."

Mirroring his nod, I say, "I hear admitting it is the first step to recovery."

He plops the beer bottle down on the table with the telephone and his blunt fingers find the doorknob.

A moment later, I'm staring over his shoulder as he begins digging behind boxes, work shirts, and coats that smell like mothballs and mildew. He's still mutter-grunting to himself, but I can't hear what he's saying with his face shoved against Carhartt.

"What are you doing?" I demand.

11

A pleased noise escapes him and he draws back, bringing with him a very familiar black bag. Instinct kicks in, screaming for escape, and I'm staggering backwards before I realize that, really, there's nothing to be afraid of. Despite that, I remain pasted—back against the yellowing wallpaper. I know that bag. That bag is *bad*.

Grinning, Cutter grabs at the bottle with his free hand and swings back toward the kitchen, shutting the door with his foot as he goes. I follow, mute and horrified yet unable to turn away, as he crunches over the broken glass from the other beer bottles.

First the beer goes down on the table *clack* and then the black bag *thunk*. Smiling ear to ear, Cutter strokes the cracked leather with callused hands. "Did you miss me, baby?"

I wrinkle my nose. "Get a room." His little eccentricities have always grossed me out and, for some reason, joking about his creepy relationship with that bag and its contents makes me feel better.

His fingers find the clasps and before I can properly prepare for the horror, the bag is opened and I'm greeted with things I had hoped I'd never see again.

The Blade Sisters. That's what he calls his little collection. Each one has a name. He made certain that I learned every single one intimately. I know every name, every serrated tooth, every finely honed edge, every possible pain that The Sisters can produce.

A shudder skitters down my spine, sending goose bumps to forgotten flesh. I glance down at my arm and a desperate laugh fights its way into my throat. If this were another time and place, I would be cowering in fear. I swallow the sick humor and glare back at Cutter. I don't have anything to fear anymore. There's nothing Cutter or The Sisters can do to me that they haven't already done.

They've already broken me. Already bled me dry. Already changed me beyond recognition and left me for dead. Already chained me to them in a way that I can't break.

And now they've moved on, leaving me with the memories and the scars and the inability to break away.

I wish I could leave them; wish I could just walk away. But walk away to what? I can't go back to being the Corey Rossi I once was. My own parents wouldn't even know me now.

I have to stay here. There is nowhere else to go.

He lifts Ethel and turns her so that she glints in the light. She's cleaner than the last time I saw her, but she's still a little rusty around the edges. Cutter holds her intimately close to his broad chest and whispers, "You hungry, baby?" Lifting a finger, he tests it against her blade then draws back with a wince and examines his thumb.

A crescent of bright blood wells on the dry pad. He sucks it for a moment, then grins like the Mad Hatter. "Good girl. I like it when you've got a little fight. I like it when you're hungry."

The way he talks to her like he'd make hot, passionate love to her if he could makes my skin crawl.

Uneasy, I glance between him and Ethel. "W-What are you planning?" My voice is shaking. Am I scared?

Yes. Even now, when I know he won't hurt me anymore, I'm terrified of Cutter when he has a blade in his hand.

Humming to himself, Cutter packs Ethel back with her sisters and shushes them as if hearing silent cries for attention. With one last stroke to the black bag, he shuts it tight. "Soon, pretty girls." His fingers pat the leather. "Soon."

I narrow my eyes at him. "Cutter." I draw it out in wobbly admonishment, like how mom used to sound when she knew I was hiding something. I think I know what he's thinking and it makes my stomach churn.

I can't let him do it.

Not again. Not to someone else. Never.

Cutter picks up the beer, chugs it, then slaps the bottle down on the table with a loud "Ahhh."

I step in front of him and hold out my stupid, useless hands. "Cutter. Let's think about this. Let's be logical," I begin, but he's not listening. He never is. He turns away from me and grabs the keys for the van off of the hook.

"Damn it, Cutter, listen to me." Desperate, I lunge at him, trying to knock him over, trying to steal away the keys. Nothing. It's like I'm not even a gust of wind to him.

I hammer and punch at him as he makes his way toward the door, scream and plea as he wades through the tall grass toward the van—which he hasn't touched in months.

I pummel the grimy window as he starts it up and run after it as he accelerates down the driveway and out onto the back road.

He doesn't hear me.

He doesn't feel me.

He doesn't even see me.

And I hate him all the more for it because he *should*. I'm here because of him, aren't I?

I follow the car out to the main road and stand there, staring after it. Cars pass me, but no one bothers to notice the kid in the dark blue jeans and red Henley standing in the median. My heart is pounding and I'm breathing hard...even though I don't have to. I'm even shaking, despite the hot summer air.

I'm afraid. Even now, I'm afraid. I know this kind of reaction is normal for an eighteen-year-old boy, but I'm not a normal eighteen-year-old boy.

Not any more.

At this point, I should be invincible. Nothing should faze me. But this does. Cutter does. The Sisters do. What they do together does. It makes me want to both cry and punch something. I hate that feeling.

Balling my fists, I scowl at the red glare of the van's lights disappearing in the distance. "I won't let you do it, Cutter!" I scream after him. "Not again! Over my dead body!"

And then a desperate laugh breaks free and I can't stop myself.

# Two:
# Mia

"So..." John's breath lands hot on the back of my neck while he follows me out of the YMCA.

As I punch through the door, I glance over my shoulder and meet his hazel eyes. "So what?"

For a moment, he seems lost. He's staring at me again. He does that. I let him, waiting until his brain reconnects. His lips twitch at the corners, flashing a slight, crooked smirk. "Do you have a date to Ti's party?"

Stopping short, I turn to face him. The first door closes behind him, trapping us in the air conditioned foyer. "Party?"

His head cocks, chocolate hair brushing his forehead. I resist the urge to brush it out of his eyes. I shouldn't do things like that anymore. Only girlfriends or girls who want to be girlfriends do things like that, and I'm not either of those. Not to John. Not anymore. Still, the urge is there—the habit like breathing.

"Tonight's party?" he says, as if that's supposed to jog some kind of memory. It doesn't, so I stare at him blankly. His straight brows knit. Such perfect, expressive brows. They're one of the first things I loved about him. "She *did* invite you, didn't she?"

Ti not inviting me to a party? Unheard of. Ti even *having* a party is unheard of. I look away from John's concerned expression and let out a little laugh, trying to pretend like the idea of being forgotten by my best friend doesn't bother me. "She probably just forgot. You know how she is."

John's expression says he doesn't buy my theatrics. He knows me too well. His hand detaches from his duffel and lifts toward mine, but I reach up and grab at my necklace, trying to reject his advances without hurting his feelings. "So, what were you asking about again?"

His hand drops back to his bag, long fingers lacing around the strap so that the knuckles turn white. "Do you want to go with me?"

Agreement leaps up from my stomach, into my heart and up to my lips, but I bite it back and force myself to think. I need to be better about not going everywhere with John. If I'm with him all the time, people will think we're still dating. It's bad enough that we still do this everyday—swim practice with my ex-boyfriend, each one of us coaxing and coaching the other to reach for the stars...it's like we never broke up.

"Um..." I breathe. Why is this so hard? Every time I turn him down, it feels like I'm breaking up with him all over again. I hate seeing the hurt in his eyes when I reject him, so I turn away as I drop the bomb. "I don't think that's a good idea." I hold my breath. Why does my chest hurt?

"Oh," he says, voice level and quiet.

17

I glance back at him. Bad idea. Now I'm caught in those dark eyes of his. He holds my gaze as he leans forward and asks, "Why?"

Why.

He asked me the same thing when I broke up with him.

The answer is the same: *Because I love someone else.*

Do I? Do I even know what love is? I grip my necklace hard, trying to force myself to be firm with him. It's difficult because John makes me want to make him smile. I love his smile and I almost never see it anymore. I miss it and I can't help but think I'm the one who made it go away. I know I am. I know how much John loves me. I don't deserve it, not after hurting him the way I did.

I finger the charm on my necklace, trying to keep my courage. "You know why," I mumble. "I told you when we broke up."

"Because there's someone else." The skin under his eyes pinches tight—like his voice.

Is he angry? Hurt? Annoyed? Jealous? I don't know. I liked it better when he told me how he felt about things, but he doesn't anymore. Despite the fact that we agreed to stay friends, things are different between us now. We don't treat each other the same and I miss that, too.

I take a deep breath and let it out slow, trying to calm my racing heart. Why does my face feel so hot? "John, I—" I start, but I don't know what to say.

Shaking his head, he straightens and looks away, hooding his eyes behind thick, dark lashes. "Never mind," he mumbles. "I don't know why I bothered asking." He angles away from me and reaches for the bar on the door.

Sudden panic grips me and before I know what I'm doing, I'm reaching out and grabbing his arm. "John!"

He goes still, his bicep flexing under my fingers as he glances down at me. A memory rushes up out of the scrapbook of my life. A dark night when I felt these same warm muscles. When I knew John's body for the first time in a more intimate way. It makes heat pool in my stomach and my face feels hotter. I'd forgotten how much I love to touch him.

For a long, stupid moment I stare up at him, mouth open. He stares back, and his expression moves from hard to soft and suddenly I sense both of us leaning toward each other—doing what we always did, giving in to the magnetic force between us.

And then, my brain catches up with what's going on. Taking a step back, I let my fingers slide from his skin and look away. "I'm sorry."

For a second, he just stands there. I can feel his eyes on me, can feel him turning hard again. "Yeah," he says, "me, too."

Hot summer air washes over me as he slides out the door. I let it close and wait for a long time in the foyer.

\*\*\*

"Mia!"

I spin on my heel in time to see Tiana running down the parking lot steps after me, her hair flying out behind her so that it sparkles in the hot summer sun. I force my grey feelings about John away and wave at her. "Hey, Ti."

She comes clattering to a stop in front of me, then bends and puts her hands on her knees, breathing heavy. "Oh," she gasps, "I was hoping I'd catch you before you left."

Hiking my purse over my shoulder, I give her downturned head an endearing expression. "I'm not going anywhere. Catch your breath before you pass out."

She nods, her head still practically between her knees.

"You know," I say, "you could have just called me. It's not like I don't answer the second your chime goes off."

She straightens and makes a sheepish expression. "Oh, right." Then she giggles. "I guess I wasn't thinking."

I smirk. Sometimes Christiana Mendez just doesn't think. She's a live-in-the-moment kind of girl and sometimes she gets a little too over-excited. She's the complete opposite of me—who thinks of all possible scenarios, makes lists, and prepares for everything days in advance. I suppose that's what makes us such a balanced pair of besties.

She straightens, her face brightening like a burst of sunshine. She's one of those people. The light in the room. Addictive to be with. Makes everyone happy. She's been that way since the first day her personality dragged me into her gravitational pull in kindergarten. I've been her best friend ever since. "I knew I'd find you here."

I push my damp hair back behind my ear; it's still wet from my shower after my daily set of laps with John. Self conscious, I shrug. "You don't win States sitting around."

"You two work too hard," she says with a smirk, then she glances around. "Speaking of, where's John?"

I blanch. "Oh, uh...he had to go somewhere."

She drops her shoulders. "You didn't get in a fight again, did you?"

I frown at her. "No, not really," I lie. *Was it a fight?* "Why do you care? You're the one that told me to drop him like a ton of bricks in the first place."

Her chin dips down once in agreement. "Totally. You're hot and young. No need to tether yourself to one man for your whole high school career. The way you two were going, you would have been married next summer."

"Funny," I say, tapping my chin. "That's not what you said originally. You said I should break up with him because I was crushing so hard on Will and should," I finger quote her, "'totally go after that sweet ass.'"

"Oh!" she says, her eyes slipping away. "Right. I did say that, didn't I?"

I frown at her, certain that her odd expression verifies my fears that she's hiding something. "Is there something you want to tell me?"

She turns back to me and blinks, "Tell you?"

"Yeah," I say, purposely looking vexed. I put my fists on my hips, pretending to be terse. "Something about a party?"

Her eyes go wide and for a second she looks like I just punched her in the gut. Then she practically explodes with excitement. "Oh, right! Thank you for reminding me. That's why I came, actually. I was gonna have a party tonight, you wanna come?"

I blink at her, glad that she finally remembered to invite me (grumbles a little bit), but still a little stunned. I had almost hoped that John was lying to me because I can't fathom Ti throwing a party. "What about your mom?" I know Ti's mom would never be okay with a party.

She shrugs. "She's not home, remember? She went to go see Uncle Tito."

I cross my arms, playing the responsible, voice-of-reason friend that I am. "You know she wouldn't be cool with this."

Tiana flashes her winning smile and puts her hands together in prayer. "That's why you have to help me make it totally awesome. It's the one chance I have to throw an amazing party. Luca's even in. He's getting the booze."

I roll my eyes. Luca is Ti's older, even stupider brother. He's a total letch and I'm sure his motive for providing alcohol to underage high school girls is something entirely other than being brotherly. *Be still my beating heart.* "Luca? Seriously? Why don't you just *invite* the cops to your party, Ti?"

She makes a mock disgusted noise and shoves my elbow. "Could you be any more of a downer?"

"I donno," I say with a smirk. "Probably. Should I try?" I touch my chin in dramatic thought. "Where should I start? Alcohol poisoning or Roofie rape? They're both such compelling topics."

"Come on!" Ti reaches out and grabs my wrist, tugging my hand away from my chin and dragging me closer to her so that I can smell the Selena Gomez perfume on her dark skin. She drops her voice. "John's gonna be there."

"Yeah, I know." And that's kind of why I don't want to go.

"*Everyone* from the team is going to be there."

That tickles my interest. "Everyone? Like...Will?" I don't retain my hope.

Her fingers tense on my arm and she grins, even bigger. "Sure. Him, too." She sounds almost...disappointed to report it. That's to be expected. She always rolls her eyes and tunes out when it comes to me crushing on Will.

I think she's jealous of the attention I give him? Or sick of it? Maybe she's worried that I'm going to be a total drag all night because I'll be drooling over him the whole time. *Mental note: spend some quality time with the bestie.*

"You sure he's coming?"

Mouth tense, she nods.

Gah, why doesn't she just dangle a chocolate cupcake in front of me? William Carrig is only like the hottest, coolest guy in New Jersey. He's smart, athletic, could probably be a Calvin Klein model, and I've been crushing on him for forever. And damn Ti for knowing it. I give a sigh of resignation and glance at the sky. "God, help me."

Realizing she has won, Ti perks up and says, "You better be praying he's gonna help you find something hot to wear by tonight."

Smiling, I pull away once more. "I'll get on that." She knows me well. There's a reason I prepare for things days in advance. Springing an invite on me just hours before a party featuring William Carrig is cruelty at its best. I need to get home and start putting together an outfit.

Remembering home reminds me that I'm already late to pick up my little sister from summer school. I start backing away from her, intent on my car because leaving Sydney alone in the school parking lot with her drop-out buddies usually leads to my car smelling like the bottom of a hash pipe. And I *do not* want to go to the party smelling like ass.

She takes a step toward me. "Wanna go to the mall? Pick out a new shirt?"

I continue backing up because if I stop, I'll fold. Who doesn't want to go shopping for a cute new outfit? And shoes? "Can't. Gotta pick up Syd and take her to her therapy appointment."

23

"I really need to talk to you about something."

Crap. I stop backing away, glance behind me then back at her. "Can it wait?"

She scrunches her brow, her bright face troubled.

I mirror the expression and step closer. "What? Is something wrong? Are you okay?"

She stares at me for a long, confusing moment. It's not like Ti to have trouble talking about anything. Finally, she closes her eyes and shakes her head. "Oh, never mind. It will take too long. It's not important."

I bite my lip. "Ti..."

She forces a smile. "I'm okay. Seriously."

Unconvinced, I don't move.

Ti huffs. "Mia. It's fine. Go get Sydney. I don't want to deal with your mother getting all mad that Syd missed her appointment." She rolls her eyes as she says this, indicating that she's not short on humor. "I'll see you tonight? We'll talk then?" Her brows lift in suggestion. Smiling, I step forward and give her a quick hug.

"Couldn't keep me away for the world." I turn away and as I trot toward my car, I call back to her. "I'll be there, I promise."

# Three:
# Sydney

"All I'm saying is that I think Kerouac is a genius," Matt is saying.

Nick rolls his eyes as he dusts cigarette ashes to the ground. "Spare me your fan-girl fodder, Matt."

"Ah come on," Matt says, his bloodshot eyes glancing expectantly between me and Nick. When neither of us responds, he drops his own cigarette with a sigh and stomps it under one of his Birkenstocks. "Whatever. I gotta get home. See you tomorrow."

I wait until he's in his car and driving away before I finally let myself relax. "Finally," I breathe, "I thought he'd never leave. I know he's your friend but seriously, he's-"

"Pretentious?" Nick offers, grinning at me behind his fingers as he takes another drag.

I grin back. "Exactly." I look away, examining the mostly empty parking lot for Mia's silver Nissan. Still nothing. Uncomfortable in the intense heat, I shift butt cheek to butt cheek, trying to unstick my shorts from my thighs.

Nick finishes his cigarette and drops it to the asphalt, letting it burn out between our feet. "She's late today," he reflects.

I nod, it's too hot to talk much. And we don't really need to talk. The quiet comfort between Nick and I is how I know things are right with the world. I finish my own cigarette, burning it down to the filter before flicking it against someone's car.

"I'm starving," Nick reflects.

Biting the inside of my lip, I mull around in my side-bag with the Wisdom Eyes on it, searching for something to nibble on. I dig down deep, past the lighter and the bowl and that hemp bracelet that I keep meaning to put back on but never do.

I've usually got—ah! "Here." I hand him one of the mostly-smashed fortune cookies from the Chinese we got last week when we were studying for our English test. I bought it, of course. It was the least I could do for him since he practically failed on purpose to be with me during summer school. He knows I'd never pass without him there to light a fire under my ass. I feel awful that he does things like that, he could be in honors if he wanted—go to an Ivy League. But, at the same time, I kind of like it.

Nick unwraps the cookie, dumps the crumbs into his palm and chucks them into his mouth. As he chews, he looks at his fortune and his full mouth turns down.

"What does it say?" I try to see it, but his large hands block most of it and what I can see of the red print is indecipherable in the bright light.

"Great misfortune awaits you."

"In bed," I add.

He narrows an eye at me, calculating. "These things are never right."

"You never know. I know where you sleep. One of these days I might decide to shank you." I elbow him playfully.

He squirms away and bats at my arm. "What's yours?"

I turn my attention to my own cookie, carefully opening it and taking only about half of the crumbs out and chewing them before fishing the folded paper out of the clear cellophane. I always eat half the cookie before I read the fortune. I don't know why. I swallow and look down at the fortune.

"You see things that others can not." I grimace.

"In bed," Nick breathes in my ear.

I give him a deflated expression and he smirks at me playfully. "Don't you think that's wildly ironic?"

"I don't think that's the proper use of the word, for one," I mutter, turning away. "Plus, I don't appreciate being teased."

Nick leans closer and presses his face to my shoulder, nuzzling my neck. I squirm away and he gives me a hurt look. "Oh come on, Syd. It's kind of funny, right?

I turn and stare at him. Why he thinks any of this is funny is beyond me. "Funny? Seeing my dead grandmother hovering near my bed is not funny." Nor is the fact that no one believes me. No one ever has. Not my parents or my friends or my sister or the doctors. "Being psychotic is not funny. Having to take all this medicine that makes me fat and sick isn't funny."

Nick breaks eye contact, looking properly ashamed of himself. "You're right. I'm sorry."

I bite back the thousand other reasons why nothing is funny and scowl at the ground. "I didn't ask to be like this, you know."

"I know." A few moments of tense silence pass and Nick makes the effort at changing the subject. "Aren't you going to eat the rest?"

I hand him the little cellophane bag in answer. I don't take the subject change bait. Instead, I ask the same question that is constantly whirling in my mind. "What if it were true?"

"What?" Nick's voice is confused.

I nibble at my tongue ring. "What if I really saw things that others couldn't?" I make sure to keep things in the past tense, the last thing I need is for anyone to think I'm still seeing things. The medication seems to, thankfully, be doing its job.

His silence makes me glance up at him and meet his blue eyes. "What do you mean?" There's only seriousness in his voice and his eyes now.

"What if I'm not really crazy? What if I can actually see things other people can't?"

Nick stares down at me, his expression so intent, so piercing, that I almost let the secret slip. I almost tell him that I don't think I'm crazy at all. I don't believe what I see is a lie my brain tells myself. I believe I really can see things that others can't.

But I don't speak. Instead, I just hold his gaze and try my best to focus on the things I know are real. He's real. I'm real. The bench we're sitting on is real. The seagulls above and the salty sea breeze are real. There are no ghosts. There are no disembodied voices, no cold hands, no idle movements from inanimate objects. I tell myself for the thousandth time that what I experienced wasn't real. It was imagined—part of a psychosis that I've lived with for years. I'm crazy. They're right. Because if it was real, then why does the medication make it go away?

I say these things like a mantra, hoping that one day I'll wake up believing it. But I don't, not really. Because I don't think I'm crazy.

"Is there something you want to tell me?" Nick asks, cautious.

I realize the dangerous territory I'm in—too close to confession, too close to being lectured and told I need to go back to the doctor. Nick means well, but I know I can't trust him when it comes to my schizophrenia, he cares too much about me to not do anything about it.

I smirk and look away. "It's nothing," I dismiss, but then words come out anyway, "It's just that...I donno. Sometimes I wonder what it would be like if what I saw—used to see—was actually real. What would happen?"

"Oh, I see," Nick's voice turns light again. "Hmm...that'd be some scary shit."

"I guess so."

Nick leans into me. "Only you would wonder something like that."

I scoff to myself and shove my dreads behind one ear. "I know. I'm sorry. I'm weird I guess."

"I like it," Nick declares, placing a paw-like hand on my head in a pat. "You've got a beautiful, chaotic mind and I love that you want the whimsical things your brain makes up to be real. I'm sure it would all be lovely."

I think back on the many things I've experienced throughout my life and decide that if I am imagining all of it, I have a very dark and frightening mind indeed. But it's nice he thinks such puppy and rainbow things of me anyway. I feel my cheeks heat and sink a little under his heavy touch.

His hand slips down my hair and fingers the bones along my spine. "I think," he ventures, "that there are plenty of things out there that we can't see. Maybe whole parallel universes."

"You're just saying that to make me feel better."

"No, I'm saying it because it's true. It's possible that maybe you do see things, Syd. And we just don't understand it yet."

Nodding, I say, "And none of you ever will. Shame, no Loch Ness Monster or Big Foot for you."

"They say seeing is believing. Maybe believing is seeing," Nick hypothesizes, his hand finally settling on my butt, his thumb sliding into my belt-loop. "They talk about that all the time, right? You know, like kids can see things we can't because we've all moved to a mindset where we no longer believe. That by telling ourselves that something isn't real, we actually make it so that we can no longer perceive it. Something only exists if we all say it does."

He's just saying all that to make me feel better about bringing it up in the first place. This is how he works. So I groan and say, "Now you're starting to sound like Matt," to shut him up.

But maybe he has a point. Maybe I had the sight and it's not the medicine at all that made me stop seeing. Maybe it's the fact that no one believed me, so I started not to believe even myself. Even now, when I say I don't believe them, some part of me does. It's like I have two minds inside and they're at war. And they have been for quite some time.

Mia's car appears the next moment, stopping in front of us. I hadn't even noticed her pull into the parking lot. When Nick and I don't get up right away, she rolls the window down, glances at us over her sunglasses, and yells over One Republic. "Hel-lo, kind of on a time crunch here."

Nick and I glance at each other and, in silent agreement, we both take a little longer than usual to get into her car—just to piss her off. As soon as my door closes, her foot stomps the gas, making my head slam against the headrest.

"Jesus, Mia, where's the goddamn fire?" I bark as she squeaks around the corner. "My appointment isn't for another hour."

Her platinum ponytail flips around as she checks directions before pulling onto the main road. "I called and had it moved up."

I yank the seat belt around me and snap it in, annoyed that she'd do something like that. It's not her appointment after all. "Why?"

"I have to get home and get ready."

"For what? The fucking apocalypse?" Because that's practically the only reason my Little Miss Perfect sister would ever exceed the speed limit. Well, that and a BOGO sale at Hollister.

As I put my foot up on the dash, she says, "Ti's having a party tonight. Don't do that." She swats my leg.

I frown at her, leaving my foot where it is. "Ti? Having a party?"

She grins, her perfectly straight white teeth sparkling. No gapped front teeth for her. Sometimes I hate her for having that smile. And yet, I can't seem to hate her—which makes me hate her even more. "I know! That's what I said."

Nick leans forward. "Isn't her mom a Nazi?"

Mia spares him a glance. "Why aren't you belted in?"

Groaning, Nick dissolves from my side and I hear the belt click the next instant.

"Sydney. Feet. Dash. Now."

Grumbling to myself I drop my foot and sit up straight before she starts lecturing for slouching.

She bobs her head, in approval—probably of herself and her ability to command the peons. She's so much like Mom it's disgusting.

"Mrs. Mendez is strict, yes," Mia finally says. "But she's not home and Ti is apparently moving into her rebellious phase. I don't approve."

"It's the end of days!" I say sarcastically as I drape the back of my hand over my forehead and feign lightheadedness, "Mia doesn't approve of a little teen rebellion!"

Mia scowls at me, so I stick my tongue out at her.

# Four:
# Mia

It takes three hours to find something decent to wear to the party. Something cool enough for the hot summer and being cooped up inside Ti's house, but not slutty. William could totally have anyone, but he's not into that kind of girl. He likes the cute, preppy look and goes for the demure, nice girls. I should know, I've made an intense study and have convinced myself that I am the perfect candidate. Now, if only he'd *look* at me, he'd see that we'd be perfect for each other.

I turn in front of the mirror one more time, checking myself out at all angles. Jersey girl poof with sparkly clips? Check. My engraved Tiffany necklace? Check. Adorable collared shirt with coal-grey, V-neck sweater vest? Check. Cute little khaki shorts (not too short)? Check. Sweet knee-high socks and high-heeled saddle shoes? Done and done.

My boobs look awesome, my butt looks great and I've got mile-high legs. Add the platinum sun-streaks to my blonde hair and the nice tan that hides my dusting of freckles? I'm looking pretty damn good.

Satisfied, I grab a little over-the-shoulder purse that I've already wedged with the essentials: gum, folding brush, emergency mascara and lip gloss, condoms, my cell, car keys, and my ID; and head out in search of the last necessary item: cash.

Dad's sitting at the kitchen table, tapping away at his laptop. Sydney is slumped beside him, her nose stuck in a battered school copy of *Lord of the Flies*. She lifts her eyes and stares at me from under a mop of dirty blond dreads. "I thought I smelled something funny."

I cross my arms and lean against the doorway. "Haha," I say sarcastically. "It's called clean. You should try it sometime."

She sticks out her tongue—which she does just because she knows I think it's disgusting—flashing me with a silver barbell.

Rolling my eyes, I turn to my father and slather on the golden girl charm. "Daddy?"

He doesn't look up. "Yes, pumpkin?"

I tuck my hands behind my back and go a little pigeon-toed, assuming the 'of course I'm still a virgin' stance. "Can I have some money?"

He looks up then—money always draws Dad's attention—and gives me the once over. "Oh, you look nice."

My smile comes automatically. It's not like I don't look this nice everyday—a girl has to do what a girl has to do to get noticed. But I appreciate that he recognizes my efforts. I fiddle with my necklace, looking sheepish and cutesy.

From the corner of my eye I see Sydney make a face at me. I ignore her. Hey, is it my fault that I know how to get what I want from my father? "It's for the party, remember?"

He snaps his fingers. "Right." Though, in reality, this is the first he's hearing of it. "Now, where was it again?"

34

I shrug like it's no big deal. "Ti's house."

He lowers a shocked brow. "Mrs. Mendez is letting Christiana have a party?"

Eager, I nod. I convinced myself long ago that if I don't make any noise when I lie, it's not really lying. "Luca is going to be there to chaperone."

Dad purses his lips, making his cheek and jaw bones look even sharper than they already are. "You know how I feel about Luca."

Smiling, I roll my eyes. "He's a good for nothing Guido. I know, Daddy."

He cocks his head and runs his hands through his silver-grey hair. "Have you asked your mother?"

Crap. I hate when they do this. It's like parents are required to share a hive-mind or something. No one is allowed to do anything unless they both agree. "No," I admit. "I forgot to ask her before she left for spin." I did that on purpose actually, but he doesn't need to know that. I'm not stupid, Mom's the bad cop.

He frowns.

"But I promise I'll check in every hour." I pat my purse. "I've got my phone, fully charged. And I'll be good." I smile, knowing that will help. I'm the trustworthy daughter, after all.

Sydney makes a disgusted noise and turns gun-metal blue eyes on our father. "You don't buy this shit, do you?"

Dad cuts his eyes at her, the expression looking more severe behind his glasses. "I believe people when they've proven to be reliable and well behaved. And don't use language like that, young lady."

She lifts her chin, her expression petulant. It's not hard to be perfect when you've got a sister like Sydney. Besides having a long history of mental illness, she lies, cheats, steals, dresses like a hobo, and is one of those people whose life revolves around a dime-bag. I'm pretty sure my parents think she's the Anti-Christ. But really, she's just a rebellious fifteen-year-old. She's looking for attention and a way to numb the pain. She'll grow out of it. At least, I hope so.

Sydney rolls her eyes and mutters, "It's only 'cause you don't catch her. She may look like a dumb goodie-two-shoes, but she's manipulating you."

*Moi? A manipulator? Well, I never!* It's not my fault I'm smart. If she'd learn to play the system, she might know what it's like to live a life free of groundings, too.

I plant my fist on my hip and give her a disapproving glare. "Shouldn't you be reading for *summer school* or something?" I mean it as a barb and she takes it like one.

Blinking like I've slapped her, Sydney wrinkles her nose and glances at our father, expecting him to stick up for her but he doesn't.

I shouldn't remind my sister she failed English. It's mean to say to someone with such low self esteem and I should be mature. I should recognize that Sydney has a harder time of it than most teens and be supportive.

But sometimes I can't help it, sometimes I just get overwhelmed. Being so giving and caring all the time is suffocating. Plus, I mean, come on, she offended my personal hygiene, is outing my methods to our father, and is trying to mess up my chances of hooking up with Will. That's grounds for war—no sister would let that fly.

Even so, I smile apologetically at her and grasp her shoulder, letting her know I didn't mean it. Much as we pretend to hate each other, we don't. This is all some kind of strange act she puts on in front of our parents to get attention. She'd be fine if Dad weren't sitting right here. She'd probably even ask to come...and I might let her if I could trust her not to end up passed out with her head in a toilet.

Dad reaches into the back pocket of his pressed grey Chinos and pulls out his wallet. I gave him that wallet for Christmas when I was ten and he's never gotten a new one. The junky old thing looks out of place on my cut and dry, Corporate American father. He pulls out a fifty and presses it into my palm. "I expect receipts and change."

Yup, CEO to the core. Part of me itches to ask if he wants me to fax the receipt to his secretary, but that would be pushing it.

I close my hand on the cash. "Yes, Daddy." To seal the deal, I lean over and give him a peck on the cheek, leaving behind a glossy pink smear.

# Five:
# Mia

Someone barrels down the hall, their hand over their mouth. Wrinkling my nose, I glance after them. They better make it to the bathroom before they puke all over the rug. What. A. Train. Wreck. When Ti asks me to help clean up, I'm gonna say no.

I drop my shoulders. No, I'll be nice and say yes. But only because I feel bad for Mrs. Mendez. The poor woman. She doesn't deserve to come home to the epic mess that this place is going to be in after tonight.

It's like a scene out of *Animal House*. I don't even recognize most of these people. I'm not sure what I was expecting. This is how it always happens, right? Someone let the news slip that there was a party with booze and the next thing you know, kids from ten different towns are showing up trashing the place.

I skim the crowd, searching for my target. Instead, I get John, who seems to materialize out of nowhere.

"Who are you looking for?" he practically screams in my ear. It's the only way I'll hear him, the music's so loud.

I glance up at him. He's looking pretty hot with his hair gelled up like that. Part of me wants to say I'm looking for my crush, but that would be mean. Instead, I lie. "Ti. Have you seen her?"

John looks thoughtful for a moment, then shakes his head. "Not for a while, no. You want something to drink?" He holds up a red Solo cup as emphasis.

I lift my brows, confused as to why my straight edge ex-boyfriend would be caught in possession of alcohol. "You're drinking?"

He smirks that crooked grin of his, showing off his adorable dimples, then tips the cup toward me so I can see what's inside. "It's just orange juice."

Grinning, I roll teasing eyes at him. "Guess it's too much to expect there's some vodka in that?"

He shrugs, looking sheepish and takes a sip to cover the sort of awkward tension between the two of us. I'm puzzling over whether it would be a good or bad idea to tell him he looks good when something catches my eye over his shoulder.

"No!" I yelp, pushing around John and running to stop two drunk guys dancing on the kitchen table, but the table topples and one of them falls on a chair and breaks it before I get to them. I slap my palm against my forehead. "Asshats!" I snarl.

John's already between the two of them, hauling them to their feet. "What the heck are you guys doing?"

One of the guys wrenches away from John and stumbles into me. He blinks at me as I try to hold him up. "Oh, hai!" He grabs my butt.

"Ohio yourself," I grunt, shoving at his chest.

He stays there, still staring with lazy eyes. "Aren't you that Mia chick?"

I half turn away because his beer breath could knock out a rhino, and narrow an eye at him, uncertain how this dorky-looking guy with monstrous acne knows me. "Depends who's asking."

His fingers tighten on my tush for an instant before disappearing altogether, along with most of his weight. John slides between us and shoves him a little. "Hands off."

My groper sticks his hands up in the air. "Hey man, no harm. We're just talking."

Ignoring him, John turns to me. "You okay?"

For a moment, there's this girly part of me that's all melty that John's defending my honor...and then I realize it's probably more of a territorial male thing and I get pissed.

This has to stop. I can't pursue Will if John's pursuing me. And I totally won't get in Will's pants if John's gonna be acting like this with every guy who comes near me. I back away from him, ball my fists, and scowl. "What part of 'we're over' don't you understand?" I hiss. I regret everything about what just came out of my mouth as soon as I say it—the tone, the words, my contorted face—but I don't take it back. It's harsh, but how else is he going to get it in his head? Being nice hasn't worked so far.

John blinks at me. His brows draw down and he takes a breath like he might argue back, but he doesn't. He just glares for a long, black moment before turning and disappearing into the crowd of gyrating bodies.

Groper closes the distance between us like nothing out of the ordinary just happened and shoves his hand out. "Ben Fitzgerald, we were in bio together sophomore year."

"Oh," I breathe, daintily shaking his sticky hand. "Right. You look um..." I search for the right words, since 'you look well' or 'you look good' don't seem right because I don't remember him. Is that horrible of me? Probably. I'm just being a horrible person today, aren't I?

"Taller?" he offers. "Hotter? I had glasses and braces back then. And Dan Wheeler used to shove me in my locker." He snorts an awkward chuckle.

Right. *Folks, we're dealing with a real winner here.* I force a smile and try to sound ridiculously cheerful. *Embrace the blond cheerleader within, Mia.* "That must be it!"

"So," he says, smoothing his hair back and trying to sound all smoky-sexy. "What are *you* doing tonight?"

*Not you.* I flounder for a moment, trying to think of something politically correct that will get me out of the situation. Then, I grab my keys from where they're dangling off my purse and lift them up. "Designated driver."

"Sweet!"

There's a moment of silence as Ben Fitzgerald gives me the once-over like I'm dressed like Princess Leia and smothered in chocolate sauce. I take a step back, afraid he's gonna try grabbing my butt again. "Uhm, excuse me. I think I hear my friend calling me." I turn and rush away before he can respond.

Around the corner, I do a gross-out dance. He was totally undressing me with his eyes! Why do all the dorky guys have crushes on me? My gaze drifts over the contents of the living room and I find most of the boys' swim team sitting with their Stepford groupies. William's not there. Sighing, I lean against the wall and stare at them. Is he even here? Why can't *he* undress me with his eyes? Better yet, why can't he undress me *period.*

41

A voice breaks through the pounding bass of Nicki Minaj blaring through the surround sound system. "You want it, Little Chica, go and get it."

I roll my eyes at the sound of Luca's slurring voice behind me and cross my arms against his oft wandering hands. "You're drunk, Luca. You should be locked in your room where you can't hurt anyone—including yourself."

He leans close, his arm coming over my shoulder. "No way. There's too much pussy out here. I'm getting lucky tonight."

I shrug out of his cheap cologne embrace. "You're disgusting."

He grins at me, wolfish under his thin mustache and braided hair. He looks like a cross between a gang-banger and Bob Marley. "So judgmental, Little Chica."

I avoid looking him directly in the eyes, afraid it will encourage him. "I hate when you call me that."

He lifts his shoulders. "You're my little sister's *mejor amigo,* no? What else you want me to call you?"

"Speaking of," I glance around, meaningfully, "where *is* your sister? I haven't seen her all night."

Luca grins. "Ti? Tiana's getting it on!" He crows it loud and proud, making a lewd pelvic thrusting gesture and spilling beer on my arm as he does so.

Flicking away the spilled beer, I blink at him, uncertain if he's joking or not. Tiana? My little Christiana? Getting it on? Here? In a house filled with mostly strangers? "With who?"

"Eh," Luca says. "Some jacked up looking douche with this lip ring." His fingers play against his lips, dragging drool over his chin.

"Lip ring?" I breathe. It couldn't be...could it? She wouldn't do that to me. I step forward and grab his sleeve. "Where?"

He struggles against me. "Hey, hands off the duds, *loco!*"

I let him go, but I don't back down. This time I glare into his black-brown eyes. "Luca, where?"

Luca blanches and looks away. "Upstairs. Where else you gonna get any privacy in here? Been up there for almost an hour, you know?"

Heart suddenly in my throat, I shove past Luca and stumble up the stairs. I run through the second floor, barrel into Mrs. Mendez's room—ignoring the couple making out on the bed—and shove through the closet door.

The Mendez house has an attic, a secret kind of clubhouse we used to go up and play in as kids...before Luca turned into a sleaze ball. These days, we just hang out up there—watch *Pretty Little Liar* reruns, gossip about the other members of the swim team, and have sleep overs. Two years ago, Ti's mom renovated the house and the door to the attic got barricaded into the back of her new walk-in cedar closet.

I take the stairs, two at a time. Then, without thinking, I push through the door at the top. And stop.

Tiana's head comes up, startled at the noise, and we stare at each other for a long moment. I don't even bother looking at William. I know it's him because I'd know him from my peripheral vision in my sleep.

My eyes are for the lipstick-smudged girl with bewildered brown eyes. The girl who I have known breath and heartbeat since we were four. The girl who stuck up for me when Jimmy King used to push me down on the playground.

The girl who knows I'm allergic to shellfish and that I love coffee ice cream. The girl who got me into watching *Teen Mom* and *Glee*. The girl who held my hair back the first time I drank too much.

43

The girl who made me feel beautiful after I was dumped by the first guy I really thought I loved. The girl who has known that I've liked William Carrig since freshman year. The girl who convinced me to break up with John because she didn't think it was fair that I dated him while secretly crushing on Will. The girl who told me to come to her party so that *I* could hook up with Will. The girl who has never voiced any desire for this boy whose naked body she's touching in ways only someone who loves him should.

"M-Mia," she whispers, eyes wide.

In those eyes I can see that she's not drunk or high or being held against her will or anything. This is my sober best friend encroaching on my fantasy territory. And she knows it. I can tell by her expression, by the way she glances down at Will and then back at me.

The world suddenly spins. I feel sick and disgusted, heavy and light all at once. My ears begin to buzz. Without a word, without a blink or a cry or any recognition that I've even seen or heard this horror, I turn and close the door behind me.

I go back downstairs, closing doors, ignoring people as they yell and jostle me. I cut across rooms, oblivious. This is a dream. A nightmare. I will wake up and this day will have never happened.

I did not just see my best friend in the whole world doing *that* to the man of my dreams. Didn't happen. No. I refuse.

I go outside. I find my car. I turn it on. I pull away. And I drive.

I drive and drive and drive some more. Until there's no gas and I have to stop and get some with the money Daddy gave me. I leave the receipt hanging from the pump.

And then I drive again.

Into another state.

Onto some lonely back roads with no lights and no other cars. It's dark and forlorn. Forgotten and abandoned, my only company is the radio blaring Florence and the Machine and my slow, painful tears.

My phone rings. It's Dad. I glance at the clock on the dashboard. Crap. I've missed a couple of check-ins. Well, I'm not picking up now; I don't feel like talking with him. As his call goes to voicemail, I pull over and call Sydney. She picks up on the third ring and for a moment I can hear Skrillex blaring in the background.

The music cuts and her voice is like victory. "Dad is pissed. You're so busted, Golden Girl."

I wipe at my tears with the back of my hand and try not to sound like I've been crying. I don't have the energy for her teasing right now. "I know."

She's quiet for a second; something in my voice must signal that this is no time for a ribbing because her voice drops and she says, "What's wrong?"

"Nothing," I lie. "Look, can you tell Dad I'm okay?"

I sense the consternation in her voice. "*Are* you okay? You sound like you're crying in a closet."

I dig my knuckles into my eyes. I don't even know how to begin knowing if I'm okay. I eventually settle on saying, "I will be. I just need some time. I can't talk to Dad right now."

"What happened?"

I draw a deep shaking breath and more hot tears come out. "I caught Ti with Will." I don't need to expound on that. Sydney knows me well enough to know exactly what that means.

She's quiet again for a second, then she says, "Fucking whore." I bite my lip. She continues, voice hot and angry for me. "I can't believe she did that. Well, screw her. With friends like that you don't need enemies."

45

I know she's right. But already my brain is trying to figure out what I did wrong, how I missed it. Did I make it too difficult for Tiana to tell me she liked Will, too? Did I just never listen? Never see?

"You want me to come over there and break her legs?" Sydney asks.

As more tears come, I can't help but laugh-scoff at the notion of my diminutive little sister breaking anyone's legs. "No. I'm not even at the party anymore. I left a while ago."

"Where are you?"

I glance out the window. Nothing but corn fields. No signs. "I donno. I'm just driving around feeling sorry for myself," I mutter.

"Well, I'm not telling Dad that. You know his stance on emotional driving."

Sniffling, I nod. He'd kill me if he knew I was driving this upset. I'd get a lecture about wrapping myself around a tree. As if on cue, my phone beeps, letting me know I've got a new text. God, he's persistent. "Look, just let him know I'm fine and he can stop waiting up for me. I'll be home soon, okay?"

"Yeah," she breathes in a sigh, like this is some big chore. Another moment of silence passes. "Mi?"

"Mmmn?"

She's quiet for another awkward moment. I half expect her to do something super sisterly like say 'I love you' or something. It's kind of what I want and need right now. "Um, nothing. Just...just be careful, okay?" Good enough.

I smile at her. "I love you, too, Syd." I hang up on her...and am confronted with a text—not from my father, but from Ti.

*We need to talk.*

Is that it? After three hours of waiting to contact me? No sorry? No I made a mistake? Like hell we need to talk. It's a little late to talk. What could she want to say to me now?

Oh crap, what if they're, like, going out now?

Finally, it hits me for real—the hurt and betrayal and loss. The realization that I've wasted my life on a friend who never loved me. Who would rather screw around with some guy than put my happiness first. I don't care how spur of the moment she is, some things are unforgiveable. I begin sobbing and then I begin shaking. Suddenly, a wave of nausea hits me. I stumble out to the side of the road and vomit.

Holding myself, I'm both sick and crying for a long time.

Someone stops—pulling their white van up in front of my Nissan. A voice in the back of my head flags stranger danger, but I'm too blank and mentally void to care. I don't think I can even stand up, everything inside hurts so bad.

I've lost my best friend since kindergarten. I know it's a loss, because I'll never be able to forgive her for doing this to me—for never even telling me that she was interested.

A guy in a 49ers hat appears from the other side of the van, his heavy body shadowed by the lights of my high beams. He stares at me, his expression that of a concerned looking father. He's old enough to be my father, that's for sure, and for a second I wonder if he doesn't have a little girl like me back home. "You okay?" I can hardly hear him beyond my radio screaming Muse's "Undisclosed Desires."

"Yeah." I wipe away tears and try to look like I haven't just been barfing and sobbing for the last ten minutes. I want to look believable so he'll go away and leave me to my misery.

He takes an apprehensive step toward me, his stiff body language aware of what he must seem like to me. "You sick or something?"

I shake my head. Then, thinking better of it, I nod. "Migraine. I'll be okay; I just need to let it pass."

He nods. "My mom used to get those. Terrible."

I nod again, avoiding looking at him. Even though he's trying to be friendly, I don't want to encourage him. I just want to be left alone. I hide behind my collapsed and bedraggled hair.

"You shouldn't stay out here." There's a warning in his voice.

He's right. This is stupid and dangerous. Someone could come speeding down the road and hit me or my car. I didn't even put my hazards on. "I know," I say, forcing myself to stand. "I'll go. Thank you." I turn to get back in my car.

A rough hand claps over my mouth, suffocating out my scream of surprise and double betrayal. Before I understand what's happening, I'm being drawn off my feet and something sharp bites into my neck.

And then I'm released. I stumble away from him, my hands going to my neck in search of what bit me. There's a needle sticking out of my skin—I can tell from the shape of it. I yank it out and, wide-eyed, I turn and look to the man in the 49ers hat.

He smiles at me, eyes dancing and expression pleased. "Goodnight, Little Duck."

Sobbing and gagging for breath, I turn and try to run. But the world spins around and the ground lifts out from under my feet. I stumble onto my hands and knees and sway there, confused and disoriented. A moment later, all my strength seems to ooze out of me and into the ground. I accordion into the dirt. As I face-plant, I wince and close my eyes but I don't feel the soil scrape my cheek. I can't feel anything. It's all distant, numb.

The world flips over. Dry ground becomes black sky. 49ers man is flipping me over, checking my pulse. "There we go, no more tears, no more pain. I'm gonna make you beautiful." I see more than feel him run his fingers along my cheek. "Just look at this palette. My sisters will want to paint you up real pretty."

# Six:
# Sydney

Sighing to myself, I roll off of my bed and promptly land in a pile of stuff. I make a mental note to organize things after I talk to Dad and head downstairs.

Dad is still sitting at the kitchen table, his fingers flying over the keys of his laptop. I don't think he has moved since I finished my homework and went up to my room.

I stop in the doorway and wait for him to notice me. He never notices me, never sees me—whether I'm perfect like my sister or the polar opposite. He and Mom both only ever really pay attention to Mia. I can't stand it. I've been doing really well with my maintenance phase, taking my meds. My delusions have stopped. And I am trying to stay motivated and organized. Though, my failing English didn't help any...

Just *look* at me!

He suddenly stops typing and glances down at his cell phone—which is strategically positioned beside his hand. Ready to be picked up in an instant. He stares at it, willing it to ring.

Shaking my head to myself, I step into the room. "She's fine, Dad. She just called me."

He looks up at me then back at his phone, his expression both annoyed and somehow vulnerable—as if confused that Mia would willingly call me over him. "Can't she call me and tell me that herself?"

I shove my hand under my dreads, hugging the back of my neck in discomfort. I try not to look for subtle meaning under his words. The paranoia is always there, always underneath. The fear that my parents don't believe me anymore. The sickness made me a liar, made me delusional. Even though I've improved, I'm afraid they still remember what it was like living with me when I had acute episodes. I fear they never recovered. And without Mia here as a buffer, proving that I actually matter, it's all too plain to me that my father wishes I was never born.

I take a deep breath, trying to put together a way to explain why Mia didn't call him. Telling Dad that Mia's upset about her bestie screwing her crush is practically the equivalent of talking about periods and reproduction with my Dad. "Look, she's having a drama queen moment right now. I don't think she wants to deal with you yelling at her for not checking in."

His brows crimp, disgruntled, as if offended that I'd suggest he'd yell at Mia for anything. And he wouldn't. He'd be all, "You okay, pumpkin?"

And she'd be, "Yeah, Daddy, I'm super! I'm sorry, I'm having *so* much fun, I forgot to call."

And he'd smile and say, "Well, you have fun, just don't forget to let me know how much fun you're having. Okay, pumpkin?"

And she'd be, "Okay, Daddy!" And she wouldn't call anymore for the rest of the night and she still wouldn't get in trouble.

I'm the one who would get yelled at and grounded.

51

Finally, he says, "Does she need me to go pick her up?"

Ace, Dad, your superhero cloak is showing. "No. She's not even at the party anymore."

His face closes down for a moment and I all I can think is, *He doesn't believe you.* "Where is she?"

I could tell him, but would it matter? Do truth and lies even matter anymore? I shrug and try my best to look guilty, to look like I'm lying. "I don't know."

Sighing, he looks away. The conversation is over.

I linger anyway, annoyed that, at this point, he won't even argue with me or yell at me for lying. "She said she's okay. She just needs some time alone. She says she'll be home soon and she doesn't want you to wait up for her."

He doesn't look away from the screen, the light of it shines in the lenses of his glasses—two white squares. "Okay." One stupid word. That's his cue to be left alone.

Still, I remain. Waiting and hoping for a conversation. When he doesn't say anything, I grasp for something. "Where's Mom?"

"She went to bed as soon as she got home from spin. Her stomach hurt."

I frown to myself. "I told her not to eat my leftover Chinese food. It's too rich for that new diet she's on."

He shoots me an almost disgusted glare, as if I've said something lewd. "I need to finish this report, Sydney."

And just like that, the conversation is over. Stiff with annoyance, I turn on my heel and retreat. I make sure to stomp up the stairs, to slam my door. And then I turn my music up as high as it will go. Zedd's "Clarity" bounds off the walls, ricocheting off of paintings I made in therapy and ping-ponging down to get caught in the rat's nest that is my room. Clothes, papers, half-read books, dirty dishes, discarded wrappers, stinky shoes.

I navigate toward my bed, the only halfway empty space in the room, and perch in the hollow between all the blankets, pillows, and stuffed animals. I stare at myself, reflected back from the be-stickered mirror on the back of the door. I see myself, a perfect picture of an insane, unloved girl. Beyond her hollow reflection, her paintings show the pain and the monsters hovering around her. Her disastrous room is a metaphor for her mind. And all around her, perched on the shelves to either side of her, are the chapstick-rimmed glasses and the pill bottles.

If I didn't take the pills, if I just gave up and let myself think whatever I believed—if I let myself truly believe that I'm not crazy, that *they* are the crazy ones and they're trying to only make me think I'm crazy— would I be happier? Would the girl in the mirror look normal? Would the crazy, dark things come alive from the pictures and swirl about her? I don't know. I wish I did. I wish I believed one way or another. I wish I could decide what truth was real.

# Seven:
# Corey

I sit in the garden and wait. The garden is my place, my territory. Just like the broken down house on the other side of Cutter's property is *Their* territory. They don't come here and I don't go there. We came to that silent agreement a long time ago and I have no intentions of breaking it.

Normally, the plants that I've cultivated back to life here bring me some measure of joy, but no amount of weeding or pruning will bring my sour mood out of the gutter. All I can do is hold my breath and wait among the closed-against-night flowers.

Cutter will be home soon.

Earlier, I tried destroying the black bag and The Sisters inside...but I couldn't. I tried destroying the house. Lighting a match, toppling the furniture. Everything I've tried before in my anger and hatred, but I'm simply not strong enough to do it.

I hate that about myself. All I can do is wait...and then what? Watch it happen? How will I stop him? I had more power then than I do now...

But at least now, I'm free...

*Is this freedom?*

Being stuck here? Slung somewhere between life and death?

Sighing, I turn my attention back to the small hole I'm digging. I can move the earth, can move the grass and the flowers, I can pet Delilah when she's whining because Cutter hasn't tossed anything down for her to eat in days. But I can't open the refrigerator and pull some hamburger meat out for her. I can't use the garden shears. I can't dig with the shovel. The most I can do is push the small things, and that doesn't do much—because I can't push the one thing I hope to push. *Him.* Down a flight of stairs. Out in front of a car. Push his head under the bathwater. Anything to get him dead and gone—to rid the world of him.

Headlights break over the horizon, white on the deep blue of on-coming dawn. Cutter is back.

I stand and watch him approach. Will he have what he went out for? What should I do?

I slip between my neatly planted rows of lilies and slide through the rusted iron gate of the rickety fence built around the old garden. He doesn't even look over here any more. Perhaps if he did, he'd see the flowers growing behind the wire mesh woven between crooked pipes and rotting stakes and he'd know I was here. He'd see what I've done—brought life and beauty into the ugliness of his hell. He'd see my sun flowers and my dahlias and my wild roses and know that not everything here is dead.

The van pulls all the way into the old barn, illuminating the rising shadows of rusting farm equipment for a brief moment before banishing them to forgotten darkness once more. I stand outside of the grey-rotten doors and wait as Cutter, whistling like always, gets out and comes around to the back of the van.

Dirty fists balled, I step into the doorway and try to sound ominous. "What did you do, you fucker?" It still feels good to swear at him.

He opens the back and steps close, blocking my view. And then he turns around, showing me his prize. A limp ragdoll of a human.

My chest seizes tight and I go still, uncertain what to do.

Cutter has a new victim.

The sound of the van door slamming as he kicks it closed startles me into action. I advance on him, screaming. "What the hell are you doing? You can't bring her here! You can't do this! It's wrong! Don't you understand!?" I flit around him like a bee, stinging and tugging at him, but I'm nothing to him. Barely an annoying little flea. Despite that, I harry him all the way into the house and up the stairs.

I bar his way into The Room. I want, more than anything, to prevent him from taking her in there, but he just shoves past me.

Growling in frustration, I rush after him. He drops her on the bed and she bounces like a tossed toy. I try to push her off, to get her out of his reach, but again I'm not strong enough. It's as if she's a concrete foundation stone.

Panting and sweating, I collapse next to the bed. I used to be able to bench three times my weight. This is ridiculous, how weak he has made me. It's like when he was cutting flesh and muscle from bone, he cut something else out as well. My soul. My will. There is no strength left anywhere. I'm surprised I can still stand up.

He disappears into the adjoining bathroom for a long couple of minutes. I don't follow; I can guess what he's doing. Instead, I stand up and stare at her.

Her cheeks are stained with smudged mascara. Her knotted hair and dirt and vomit-stained clothing have most likely seen better days. She's a Barbie doll that got left outside for too long. It's a grotesque picture. One that I know will only grow more and more horrific as the days drag on.

What should I do?

The shower turns on and a moment later, Cutter returns for the girl. I trail him to the bathroom, half ashamed of myself for watching but half needing to try everything that I can to stop him from doing what I fear he'll do.

I only know what he did to me.

I don't know what he'll do with a girl.

As he starts to pull her clothes off, I say, "Don't do this, you sick bastard."

He ignores me, instead taking great pains to be precise and gentle with her clothing, as if he's afraid he'll rip a seam or pop a button. It's a likely prospect considering Cutter is a friggin' Neanderthal and this girl is small and petite. He's huge even compared to me, so seeing him with her makes her look like a porcelain doll.

I watch in morbid fascination for part of it. Despite my hatred for Cutter's art, he has a certain way about him, something in his expression that one can't help but stare at in wonder. From the beginning, I've always pondered what is going through his head when he does this. What does he think he sees? What kind of sickness is this? What kind of medication could fix this?

At this point, I think the only help there is for Cutter is a bullet to the head.

When he yanks her shorts down, I snap to my senses and rush forward. "Stop it!" I shove at the shorts, trying to get them back where they belong, but he just yanks all the more harder until both shorts and panties come sliding down and I have to look away.

I cover my eyes with my hands. Like a kid. Like a guy who has never seen a female body before. Simply because it's too terrible to even think about right now. This is not the time to look or feel anything. This is against her will and I refuse to be part of anything of that nature. I turn away, abandoning him.

"You're an animal!" I howl, shoving at the Penthouse magazines stacked by the toilet. They slide across the tiles, tipping open and revealing things that I hope are not teasers of what's to come. It only inflames my hatred of him more. "You're sick!" I thrash around some more, making it known that I'm against this whole thing. The curtains scream along the rod, the towels tumble from their bars, the toothpaste falls off of the sink. "I hope you rot in hell, you fucker!" There are not words or vile conjurings of the brain enough for me to tell him what I wish upon him.

Cutter deftly folds the last of her clothes and places them in a neat pile on top of the laundry bin as if intending for them to get washed. I don't really understand why; it's not like she'll ever wear them again. Pissed at this disgusting game, I shove at those too and they fall in a heap beside the towels.

Oblivious to my tantrum, Cutter lifts the girl and drops her under the warm spray of the shower. I calm down slightly, certain that this must mean that he's not going to violate her...at least, not yet. If I stopped and thought about it, I'd know that Cutter wouldn't do anything until she was awake and certainly not without his little gaggle of glistening Sisters to watch with a thousand serrated smiles.

As Cutter begins a meticulous scrub down of the new prisoner, I sit on the toilet seat and sulk. I don't watch, I don't want to see her. That would be wrong. Despite that, the noise is enough—the constant *rasp, rasp* against her skin is like nails on a chalkboard. My brain turns it into skinning and in turn it peels me from the inside out.

I hold my breath, screaming against the held air.

A few moments later, I hear the tell tale noises of something gone awry and I have to glance over.

"Ugh! Dude!" I look away. I hate when I accidentally see that. It's bad enough with the videos and the mags, but now he's got a live specimen. A shiver crawls down my back and I say a silent prayer that Cutter's own social inabilities will keep him from physically harming this girl. What he already plans to do is bad enough, she doesn't need this kind of bullshit on top of that.

Cutter finishes himself off and gets up to wash his hands. I roll my eyes at him in the mirror. "You feel better, asshole?" His eyes come up and wander to the reflection of the girl flopped in the tub, one arm flung over the side. He makes a sharp whistling noise, shakes his head, and then turns off the water.

"You are a pathetic excuse for a man. Have you even touched a conscious woman?" I challenge.

He smoothes wet hands through his lanky hair. "Keep it together."

"Right," I say, mocking him. "Wouldn't want to blow your load just by looking at her, perv."

A moment later, he's back to scrubbing, acting like nothing happened. Though his scrubbing is a little harder, a little deeper, leaving red marks behind. It's as if he's punishing her, like it's her fault.

I feel bad for this poor girl. If he doesn't touch her again, she'll never know this moment happened. That's probably a good thing. But still, she seems irreparably sullied by this whole affair and I feel dirty for her. Just being in the room makes me feel gross and wrong, like there's maggots under my skin, as if I'm the one who should be slammed in jail and left to rot. I want to run away...but someone has to try and stop him. Someone has to be here for her.

No one was there for me. *They* weren't there for me...and they could have been.

I stare at the wall and bat at the toilet paper, making it unfurl in a massive heap on the floor. "I don't know how you live with yourself. You make me sick." I wish I could be sick. For real sick.

Ten minutes later. The prisoner is suitably clean. Even her teeth are brushed. I had knocked the brush under the radiator where he couldn't reach it, but he just scrubbed her mouth with his finger...which was worse and made me afraid to steal the towels away lest he rub her dry with his own hairy body.

He doesn't bother drying her though. Cutter wrestles her still dripping body into an old, hideous nightgown. I don't understand exactly how the outfit factors into this ritual. I assume it has some deep psychological thing to do with his mother. Isn't that how all the wacko murderers are? Bates and Gumb...they had mommy issues. I've looked for the body of Mother Cutter—in the attic, down in the basement with Delilah, in the garden. If he did kill her, he hid her well. He's good at hiding things he doesn't want found.

After she's dressed and combed, and painted up like a garish 80s punk-rocker, Cutter picks her up and brings her back into The Room. He puts her back on the bed and he reaches for the chain but I push it out of his grasp, wanting to make it impossible for him to keep her here. It works for the first and second time, but not the third. He gets smart and grabs the chain from the base of where it's connected to the brass headboard. He does the same with the rest, preventing me from further showing him my displeasure.

Once she's cuffed limb to limb, he pulls a handkerchief from his pocket and gags her with it.

Stepping back, Cutter admires his handiwork. I let out an unsteady breath. It looks painful—cold, rusted iron on golden, delicate skin, too-tight gag ripping at cherry balm lips.

Cutter says, "She'll be out for a while yet. Best let her sleep it off and figure it out. It's always better when they've had time to figure it out and build it up before making the first visit."

Stretching, he turns and disappears from the room, locking it from the outside. Just in case. I rush to her side, trying to tug at the cuffs, but all I can do is rattle them about. I pace the room, end to end, wracking my brain. What can I do? How can I help? I slip into the hall and shove the key to unlocked, but what good is that? I can't open the door and I can't unchain her from the bed, so unless she's secretly She-Hulk, an unlocked door will be little use to her.

I edge back into the room and pout at her prone form, almost pissed at her for getting caught and putting me in such a vexing situation. It had never occurred to me that it was my job to stop him, but now that it's happening, it seems that this is what I'm here for. This is why, after he released me, I stayed here in Cutter's house instead of going home.

I didn't want it to happen to anyone else. The only problem is that I *can't* stop him. So, what do I do? Just watch? Bear witness to this macabre reality as it plays out?

The girl on the bed shivers and shifts, her brow crimping in some distasteful way. I step close to her, drawn by her pain and uncertainty. What is she dreaming about? Is it worse than here? Worse than what will befall her when she lifts those long lashes?

I reach out and push at the blanket folded at the end of the bed, covering her against the chill of early morning. Covering her skin before it is laid open to the world.

# Eight:
# Sydney

"Sydney, can you go wake your sister up? She's going to be late for her practice with John."

I hear Mom, but I don't respond. I just continue staring at the back of the box of Lucky Charms and bobbing my head to DeadMau5.

I see Mom glance at Dad from my peripheral vision. "Honestly, I don't know what to do with her."

A moment later, my ear buds are forcefully removed from my ears.

"Ow!" I growl, meeting my father's angry green eyes.

For a long moment we glare at each other and I wonder why, if they hate me being plugged in all the time, they insisted I start listening to music in the first place. I know they wanted me to listen to it to drown out the voices, so I couldn't hear them whispering to me. But that comes with a price—if I can't hear the voices of the imagined people, I can't hear the voices of the real people either. It's their own fault.

"Your mother is talking to you."

I scowl at him then turn my attention to my mother. "What?"

Mom makes an obvious effort of composing her face. She's severe looking. The sharp pencil skirt, perfect silk blouse, and French twist don't help to soften her. She speaks to me like I'm both deaf and an idiot. "Can. You. Wake. Up. Your. Sister?"

"I *can*," I say back. I return to eating.

"*Will* you," she huffs, her patience for me thin.

I glance back up at her and give her the once over, mentally telling her she's got her own two legs. Two nice, shapely legs—which I did not inherit, by the way—that she spends an hour at spin every day to keep that fit and perfect. I really don't get why parents feel it necessary to delegate to their children, it only makes them more lazy. She stares at me, expectant.

I consider non-compliance. It won't help with anything, though, so I grudgingly rise and head for the stairs.

Mia's door is closed, like always. She treats her room like some kind of inner sanctum of a temple, like there's something secret and wonderful within. All she's hiding is the fact that she's not as perfect as my parents think she is. She's got half-naked guys on her walls, her room's a pigsty like mine, and I know she lost her virginity to John in there.

I bang on the door. "Wake up, Pumpkin Princess, Mummy and Daddy request thine royal presence."

No answer.

I bang again. "Mia! Wake up!"

Sighing out a guttural noise of annoyance and leaning against the door, I lower my voice to be nice. "Look, I realize you might feel like you can't show your face to the world, but seriously, you can't hole up in there forever."

I wait and wait.

"Mia?"

Nothing.

Growling to myself, I grab the door handle. "I'm coming in." I shove into the room. Immediately, the amount of color and the sharp tang of pool chlorine assault my senses. I zero in on the lump in the bed. "Mi, get up. I don't care if you're tired from coming home at the ass-crack of dawn, if you're not down there suited up and ready for laps in three minutes, Mom's gonna eat me for breakfast." I grab the blanket and pull it away.

Only Mia's not there. It's just a pile of clothes.

"Mi?" I glance around the room. Her closet looks like it exploded, but she's not in there. I wander into the bathroom we share. I come back, get on all fours and, feeling like a tool, check under the bed.

Biting my lip, I wander toward the window and part the blades. Her car isn't parked on the side of the house like it always is in the morning. Mia never came home. Mia *always* comes home.

Suddenly uneasy, I streak across the hall and close the door behind me. What to do...what to do... I pull my cell out of my pocket and call her.

It rings and rings and then goes to voicemail. I hang up. Lowering my cell, I grab the back of my neck with both my hands. Part of me is mad at her for not coming home on time, but a more primal part of me is worried. It's not like Mia to not come home. Mentally, I try to reason that there are many explanations as to why she isn't here, why she wouldn't pick up her phone. But, deep down, I know something is wrong.

*Is it?* Maybe I'm dreaming? Maybe I'm hallucinating again? I mean, this is really uncharacteristic for Mia, which means it's not real, right? And if that's the case, then I must be going crazy again...

Chest tight, I turn and check my reflection in the mirror, making sure I'm still me—I paw at my cheeks, reassuring that my suddenly burning face isn't exploding with spider pods. Panting for air, I scrutinize my room, making sure that none of the painted monsters are oozing out of the paper. I shove at the piles, making sure that there aren't snakes or rats or dead bodies squirming on the floor.

Nothing. Everything seems normal. But the panic is rising mad in my body, the blood is lava, the skin is ice, the heart is a hammer, the lungs are bellows. I'm crazy. I'm insane. It's all going wrong. I'm losing it.

I close my eyes and pinch myself, really hard. A few times. I don't feel any different. Screams fighting to claw their way out of my mouth, I grab a pen. I have to be sure, have to be certain. I can't let the insanity come back, I have to drive it away, shove it back, let it out of my body before it takes hold. I stab my leg.

The pain skewers me. Makes me yelp. I pant against it, hold my breath, let the blood drip along my fingers.

I'm alive. This is real life. I'm not insane. I'm awake. I'm all better. There is no insanity. Get a grip, Syd. I take a few breaths, wait for my heart and breathing to calm down. I open my eyes. My room is the same. I hold my breath, pull the pen out and get on my hands and knees. Taking a deep breath, I open my door, hoping to see Mia riffling through the mountain of clothes and shoes across the hall, hoping that reality has returned to normal.

No such luck.

The panic crawls back up my throat. I glance down the stairs and scream, "Mom! Dad!"

A moment later, they're both running up the stairs. They stare at me, at the blood on the carpet. Whatever my expression must say, it's not good because I haven't seen them look at me like that in a very long time. *It's not me. Don't look at me like that. I'm not insane. I'm not. This is real life.*

I point at Mia's room.

And their reactions verify that this is indeed real life. That my insanity is not just in my head. Instead, it has seeped out, and has turned my world upside down.

# Nine:
# Mia

Coming awake is like crawling out of a black hole. The light hurts my eyes. So much so that it gives me an instant splitting headache that crawls down into my intestines and makes me want to both vomit and pass out at the same time. Groaning, I roll onto my side, but something stops me, tugging at my hand. I yank back at it but it doesn't move. Confused, I try to sit up, but my other arm and legs are bound as well.

I'm trapped.

I blink around. Yellowing floral wallpaper hanging from plaster walls, hardwood floor covered in dark stains, off-white ceiling spattered with deep brownish flecks. There's a big window framed by faded blue gingham curtains across from me. There are two closed doors painted with cracked white paint. There's a bed stand and one of those hospital tables that go over a bed. I'm not in a hospital, but I am in a bed. Bound to a bed.

A twisted gasp escapes my throat.

Adrenaline pounds through my veins, making me forget the headache and doubling the sick feeling with a bout of panic. I suddenly remember last night. Was it last night? How long have I been here? And where is here?

I rattle at my chains, trying to break free. All it does is break my skin and make me bleed. I flop my head back on the pillow, breathing hard.

My heart is hammering.

I can't breathe. I'm choking on my fear.

I want to scream for help, but I'm gagged. It's probably not smart anyway. That might bring my captor faster. And who knows what he'll do to me. Ohmygod, what if he's already done something to me?

I glance down the length of my body only to find, to my horror, that I've been changed out of my clothing. Ew! He took my clothes off! Urg, what if he touched me? What if he... I wriggle around, trying to feel if I've been violated or not. It doesn't feel like I've had sex, but that doesn't mean anything. My skin begins to crawl and I break out in a sick sweat, trying hard not to vomit at the prospect of that nappy old 49ers guy on top of me.

I kick my feet in disgust, rattling my chains again. I wrench at the cuffs, tearing until the bed starts to scrape across the floor and it feels like my hands are going to come off. But nothing gives, nothing breaks. Not even my skinny little wrists. I can't get free.

I gnaw at my gag, hating the wet, itchy thing. Everything is wet and itchy. It's hot. Especially now, after I've been thrashing and freaking out. The sun is right on me. I blink into it, seeking some promise of escape, but even the window is barred.

I'm captive. Imprisoned. Bound and pressed against the poking springs of this bed. I have no idea what he's going to do to me. I don't even know where I am. How long will it take for them to find my car on that little road? Even so, what's that going to tell them? Someone kidnapped me from the side of a road in the middle of nowhere. I don't know how far he has taken me since then.

They couldn't even do some kind of *CSI* thing where they track my phone because I left it sitting on the passenger seat. I'm going to be one of those missing people that they put on milk cartons and billboards.

No one is going to find me.

And this is how I'm going to be remembered.

And I won't have even lived a life worth bragging about.

And one day, they'll find my body and I'll be the inspiration for an episode of *Bones*.

A lone sob leaps into my throat, wracking my body. And then suddenly, I'm crying and whimpering, certain that this is it.

# Ten:
# Corey

I sit in the corner and watch as my fellow inmate flows through the sudden realization and horror of what has happened to her. I did the same thing. I'm sure *They* did, too.

When she starts crying, her keens are like little knives—slicing in ways I didn't know I could be cut. It's terrible and uncomfortable. I want to get up and soothe her, calm her and tell her that I'm here for her, but what good am I, really? I can't make Cutter stop and even if I could, I couldn't free her.

Once upon a time, I thought I was strong. I figured hey, I can lift this much weight and I'm the state champion, that must mean I'm physically strong. I'm cool and rich and popular and I'm a total ace with the chicks, so that means I'm socially strong. I never cry and I always deal with whatever bullshit comes my way, so that means I'm mentally and emotionally strong.

Turns out I didn't know what strength was.

Because this girl's fate makes me cry and this girl's tears make my knees weak and my inability to help this girl makes me feel as impotent as a child.

So, I escape into the dark hallway and press myself against the wooden skeleton of walls going bald of plaster and floral wallpaper. I sink to my butt, huddling on the colorless, mite-infested, threadbare carpet. I hang my head between my knees, cover my ears with my hands, and sob in gasps of stale, dry air for her because I know—more than anyone—what's coming.

# Eleven:
# Sydney

A whole day. A whole day we have been *sitting* here. Me, held captive in the stuffy silence of baited breath, forbidden to move or do anything. Just waiting.

"Tell me again exactly what she said," Dad suddenly says.

I roll my eyes, tired and annoyed. "The same thing I just told you."

Dad frowns at me. "Again."

I close my eyes and let out a long breath. No amount of me repeating myself is going to make them believe me any more. "She called last night to ask me to tell you she was fine. She was driving around, sulking. She didn't know where she was and said she'd be home soon."

Mom scoots forward on the couch. "And this was about Tiana?"

I nod. "Mia has a crush on that guy Will Carrig, the one who does the high dive on the team?"

Mom purses her lips and scrunches her nose in response. Will's not the Ivy-bound son-in-law she had in mind for her precious Mia.

"And I guess she caught Ti hooking up with him last night or something. She was upset, so she went driving," I explain. Then add, "She said she'd be home," again, like that will drag her through the door.

Mom and Dad look at each other, then back at me. I have no idea if they believe me. Mom's eyes keep glancing down toward my leg, which makes me feel like she's suspicious that I imagined last night's phone conversation.

I hold up my cell. I've been clutching it, hoping Mia will call me back. "You can check my log. I did talk to her last night."

Mom looks away and finally decides it's time to act. "We've waited all day. What do you want to do, Pete?"

Dad bites his lip. "Well, it seems like she just wants to be alone right now. Let's wait until tomorrow and see."

"What?" I breathe. "You're joking, right?"

His gaze cuts at me.

I talk before he does. "Don't you know Mia at all?!" I whimper, tears inexplicably coming to my eyes. "Don't you know your own daughter?! Mia wouldn't just disappear. She wouldn't not call people and let them know where she was. She wouldn't ignore me and she most certainly wouldn't do something weak like run away." My sister is the smartest, strongest person I know. She always has the answers, she's logical, and she follows the rules. She is the rock.

"Something is wrong!" I howl. "You guys are just sitting here. Don't you watch TV?! Don't you know the first 24 hours are the most critical? Get off your asses and call the goddamned police!"

Dad stands then, face red and veins bulging in his neck. "Go to your room!"

74

I stay planted on the couch, scowling at him. He gives me 'the look'—that thing I hate that makes me feel like unwanted filth, like he might do something drastic like take me out back and shoot me. I glance at Mom who won't look at me. I'll get no help here.

I stand, collecting my stupid summer school book, and leave the room—but I don't go upstairs. Instead, I sit on the bottom step and listen.

After a few moments, Mom speaks. "She's right, Pete. This isn't like Mia."

Dad's quiet for a long time. "She's fine, Vicky. Can't you see that? She's just upset. You do that all the time, cut yourself off. She is your daughter."

I roll my eyes.

"I don't know," Mom is saying, voice low. "Something doesn't feel right. In my gut."

Dad's voice turns lighthearted. "You're still probably sick from that Chinese food."

Mom doesn't laugh at his joke.

I scrub my hands against my cargo capris and they leave a trail of nervous sweat. I try opening up *Lord of the Flies*, but it just makes my imagination run wild. What if Mia is lost and alone in the wild somewhere? What if she's going mad like these little boys in the book? *What if...what if... Ugh, stop thinking, Sydney!*

I'm just about to pop in my headphones to shut off the thoughts when the phone rings. I leap up, scrambling for the phone on the little table beside the front door. Dad and I practically knock heads jumping for it. Dad gets to it first.

I watch his face, expectant. I have to look away for a second, confused by the vice squeezing my hand. Mom is holding it.

I didn't even realize she'd gotten up and grabbed it. I squeeze back, confused and elated at the same time. Mom hasn't touched me in a long time.

Dad says, "What?"

I look back. And then I feel my face fall as his does.

"Yes, it's mine. My daughter was driving it last night. She didn't come home. Yes. Please." He swallows hard and gives Mom this desperate sort of expression. Her fingers go slack in mine, then disappear. She puts her hands over her mouth and makes a horrible whining noise. She disappears into my mental background as I hyper-focus on Dad, trying to hear what the person on the other side is saying, but I can only hear Dad saying, "Anything you can do. Uh huh. Yes. I'll be right there. Thank you."

I don't miss how his hand is shaking when he puts the phone down. He stares at the receiver, his glasses slowly sliding down his nose, but he doesn't notice. The silence is maddening. I can't stay still, I'll scream. I stand on weak legs and take a hasty step forward. "What?" I choke out. "What happened?"

Dad lifts his eyes, pushes his glasses up on his nose...and it's like he sees me for the first time in half a dozen years. My heart squeezes tight, choking me, stilling me. "They found her car."

I blink at him. Found her car. Just her car. *Not* her. What does that mean? "Where?"

"Upstate New York."

What? That far? Granted, it's not hard to pass through states when you live in the Northeast. I search the table, search the floor. I feel confined and useless. I don't understand. I wish I hadn't stabbed my leg, I wish I hadn't let the insanity come falling out of my body.

It's worse here in the real world than in my head. At least in my head, Mia was safe.

I voice the question that my mind keeps throwing at me. "What does that mean?"

Dad looks away and his fists ball at his sides. "I don't know."

# Twelve:
# Mia

Late in the evening, I've cried myself to numb. My skin feels hot and itchy and I've peed myself; I couldn't hold it any longer. I can hear someone from what sounds like a downstairs. They're whistling the waltz from *Sleeping Beauty*. *"I know you, I walked with you once upon a dream..."*

Well, nice to know someone's having fun.

For what feels like the thousandth time today, light and shadow wander across the room, making me feel like something is there...watching, pacing, making the curtains move...but when I look there's nothing. I must be cracking up. How long does it take for someone to go mad in situations like this? There are only so many times you can imagine your own horrible, bloody fate without it eventually making you crazy, right?

A moment later, the whistling starts coming up the stairs. I hold my breath, waiting. The door opens and 49ers guy saunters into the room.

He's dressed differently today. Now, he's cleaned up and is wearing a pair of surgical scrubs, though they aren't clean.

They're stained with blood. He's holding a big black bag, like the kind old-fashioned doctors used to have.

I feel everything inside of me shrink inward and my lungs squeeze flat in a whimper-whine. *Oh my God, this is it. I'm gonna die.*

"Well hello." He shuts the door and smiles at me, his expression everything a doctor's bedside manner should be. "I see you're awake and breathing. That's always good." He hooks his toe under the hospital bed table and loops it toward me. "Sometimes they don't always wake up. And that's no fun, is it?"

I blink at him. I don't know what to say to that. It's sick and means nothing good for me. I hear rattling by my head and realize it's me shaking in my chains.

He puts the bag on the table. "Oh, don't be scared. It will be over in no time."

A gasp garbles in my throat. *Over?*

He reaches into the bag and pulls out a huge knife. *Oh Jesus!* I squall and struggle against my bonds, terrified of what that knife might be for. Is he going to slit my throat? I wrench so hard it feels like my arms are going to pop out of the sockets.

"Ah, ah, ah," he admonishes, lifting his brows and swinging the knife up to my throat, cold and sharp. I go still instantly, my body turning cement, scared he'll cut me. "No wiggling, Little Duck. You ruin my art, you die. You got it?"

*Whoosh, whoosh, whoosh.* My blood is rushing in my ears.

Still aware of the knife at my throat, I nod my head just a little. My heart is going to explode if it beats any faster.

I feel hot and cold at the same time, like I'm being stretched in every direction until my limbs feel like they'll dissolve.

He pulls the knife away. "Good. I hate when you guys mess it up. Means I have to start all over again. You know how rare it is to finish a masterpiece? I've only done it once, you know." He puts the knife down on the table, laying it with reverence. "It makes the Blade Sisters unhappy."

I lean my sweating face against my arm, tensing everything up, and hold my breath—trying not to shake and trying not to sob because I'm scared he'll get mad and stab me. *Don't whimper. Stop it. Shut the fuck up, Mia!* I bite my lip until I taste blood.

He reaches into the bag and pulls out another one. "This one is Mary Sue." He lays her beside the other, larger one and then touches the larger one's handle. "And this is Ethel. She's the eldest, you know. She has a temper."

I blink at him through my terror tears, trying to focus beyond the shakes and hiccupping gasps. He's completely off his rocker. Well, I already knew that. Anyone who kidnaps a random person off the side of the road and holds them captive is a nutter. I close my eyes in dread. I'm gonna die. He's gonna carve me up like a Thanksgiving turkey. Is he going to go all Hannibal and eat me, too? I bite my lip because I'm beyond whimpering and beginning to moan, and my own noises of terror disturb me most.

He continues speaking, introducing me to the whole clan of blades. Ethel, Mary Sue, Big Bertha, Nadine, Mavis, Polly, Donna, Pearl, and Little Evie Lee. By the time he finishes laying out his arsenal of torture, I've peed myself again—a hot pool against my icy skin—and my chest is hitching so fast from imagined fantasies that I couldn't breathe if I wanted to.

Which I don't. I want to die right here, right now. Make it so he never touches me with those monstrous things he calls Sisters. I start gagging.

Almost as a reflex, he reaches out and pounds on my chest with a big meaty fist. Pain blossoms across my breast and I draw a sharp screaming breath. My body remembers the taste of oxygen and everything tingles and stings anew.

"Now, the question is," he says, lifting Pearl and running his fingers over her namesake handle, "who gets first blood?"

I shake my head and whimper at him, new tears coming to stinging eyes. This is a nightmare. This is too horrible to be true. I have to wake up! What do I do? Beg? Plea? I try speaking to him, my voice coming out in high-pitched muffles behind the gag.

"Heh?" he says, leaning forward. "What's that? Speak up, girl, you're yowling like a cat."

I try to slow my words, try to be clearer, but I'm too panicked. "Please don't kill me, mister, I'll do anything you want! Anything!"

He shakes his head and speaks down to Pearl. "Kids these days, they don't know how to speak proper English." He puts her down and runs his hands over the blades. He circles the table a few times, feeling up each in turn as if she were a lover and humming the *Sleeping Beauty* song again. Finally, his fingers stop on Big Bertha...or was it Mavis? I can't remember.

49ers guy looks up at me and he lifts the blade, a wicked serrated thing. "Mavis has volunteered to show your maiden flesh how real art is made."

I suck in a breath, my muscles so tense that I feel like I'm going to snap.

"But," he says, putting her down, "Little Evie Lee knows how to be precise and gentle in the difficult places.

She is most humble and never takes the credit she deserves." He strokes Evie Lee reverently then turns to me. "Are you ready for her kiss?"

I scream and thrash anew, desperate as a mad woman. It's the last thing I can think to do other than passing out. I want to pass out, but for some reason I'm apparently not a fainter. This totally blows.

"Enough," he says.

I don't stop.

Something comes down hard against my face, making pain explode and ricochet from one side of my head to the other and back again. I gasp, feeling like the black light is going to overcome me, but then it fades back, drawing the pain into a place of sting and pulse. I blink, startled.

49ers guy straightens and cradles the back of his hand. "Behave yourself and we'll get along fine." His eyes rove over me and he frowns. "You've been struggling. That's no good. No good at all, Little Duck. You'll damage the canvas."

Moving away, he bends and removes several rolls of gauze from the black bag. As he comes toward me, I try to cringe away, try to draw into myself lest he strike me again, but there is only so much cringing and defensive balling one can do when chained spread eagle on a bed.

He sits beside me. He smells like sweat and dirt and something I can't describe, something that reminds me of funeral homes. Grabbing my arm, he examines my wrist for a moment before shoving the gauze in and out of the cuffs, roughly wrapping it around my wrist.

He whistles as he continues on, wrapping bloody wrists and ankles, though it probably doesn't matter. I probably have tetanus now, not that I'll live long enough for it to matter.

"There we go, Little Duck, all nice and wrapped up. Now," his hand wanders down my thigh and grasps at the ugly little nightgown he dressed me in, "let's see what we have to work with."

He shoves my nightgown up over my hips.

Instinctively, I try to clamp my legs together and blush hotter than the sun, turning my eyes away in shame. He starts poking and prodding at my legs.

"A little skinny," he muses, voice distant and calculating. "Nice shape though, lean muscles."

I glare at him. No one asked for his opinion and if he doesn't like it he can most certainly go get another pin cushion. I try to wriggle away, but he slaps my leg so hard it stings. "No moving! We're working here!"

I go still again, moaning in distress. *Please don't, please don't.*

He glances up at me, his expression a hungry one that I don't like. "Are you embarrassed to show me?" His hand wanders up my thigh and his fingers slip between my legs. I whimper. *Not this. Anything but this. Please, please, please, Mia, wake the hell up!* "You shouldn't be." His fingers press against me, rough and dry, horrible and invading. "Your skin is beautiful."

Suddenly, the table with all the knives comes streaking forward, slamming into my captor. The knives spill out and clatter onto the floor. His hand slides away, called to the aid of his fallen Sisters. Next thing I know, my nightgown is being shoved back down, as if the air itself wished to preserve my decency.

49ers man straightens, knives in both hands, and starts to laugh. "Are you jealous!?" he bellows. "You want some of it? Or are you mad I never touched you like that?!"

The curtains whip up and billow, a chair streaks across the floor. Little Evie Lee goes skittering out of the room. "You little bastard," 49ers yells.

Dropping the knives, he turns on his heel and runs after the animate Evie Lee. "You come back here with Evie Lee! I need her!"

And just like that, I'm left alone with the Blade Sisters and my pounding heart and my utter horror that I'm going as bat-shit crazy as my sister.

# Thirteen:
# Corey

I bat Evie Lee all the way to the cow pond. Cutter still thinks she's hiding in the tall grass so while he's yanking up half the yard looking for her, I book it back into the house and head up to The Room. I bustle about, trying to hide each of the Blade Sisters from Cutter before he returns huffing and sweating to the doorway.

I run with Polly while I've got her. I take her to the garden and bury her under my begonias. I'm tamping the dirt down, grinning in satisfaction with myself, when I hear screams from The Room. Delilah starts barking, adding to the horror of the moment.

My stomach sinks. Cutter started without Evie Lee and the other Sisters. I was certain I'd taken the most important sisters first, certain that he couldn't go on without his specialists.

But perhaps it doesn't matter to Cutter now. Perhaps he's just that starved an artist. Perhaps his muse has driven him past the brink of insanity, riding his back and whipping him with a steel-tipped flogger.

I look up at the murky window, desperate. I want to go to my fellow captive, hush her pain, tell her it will be over soon and the pain will eventually disappear. I want to tell her to just let go, to die and let it all slip away—to be the paint peeling off the siding, to let her bones droop like the foundation, to fall into ruin, collapse into herself, be far away and distant, to die in silence...and not to let Cutter win.

I want to go back up and physically stop him. I want to punch his face in until his brain oozes out of his empty eye sockets, to skin him alive so he can know what it feels like. I want to somehow make the blades disappear like I've already done with half of The Sisters already. Take away his tools of insanity. But would it matter? Would he just go find a pair of scissors or a kitchen knife?

She screams again, high pitched, long and wailing. Delilah howls with her, though I'm certain Delilah's howls are those of glee. That dog was made by Satan himself. She and Cutter are a perfect pair. I ball my fists.

Besides...

More screams and Cutter laughing in glee. He's a crazed Ring Master, driven wild by the circus of gore, the three rings of the looping designs he carves into skin, the endless parade of blood and torture.

I begin to shake.

Besides...useless.

I close my eyes, but all I see are the designs and his grinning mad-man face. My own memories, my own pain.

Besides...helpless.

I can't see it. Not again. Not from the outside looking in.

I turn away, blocking the grey death house out of my vision.

It's too close. Too frightening to do again.

Instinct comes into overdrive; I turn and I run from Cutter's insane artistry. I run like I never got to do before, until I burn all over and there is no air. And then, panting, I sag to the ground and sob for my own weakness and for the girl I left behind. Because no matter how far I run, I just can't escape the sound of her screaming or the mental images of blood. Dripping, dripping, dripping. Across shredded skin and onto the floor.

Someone touches my shoulder. It's one of *Them*. She looks down at me, childish face grave, and shakes her head at me. I look away, understanding now why no one came to help me. Even though the others knew, they didn't come. Because there is nothing we can do.

# Fourteen:
# Sydney

Nick passes the joint to me. I lift it to my lips and take a deep one, desperate for the escape and relaxation. As it settles into me, I let out a shaky breath. Nick's fingers find mine and pull the joint away.

"They're gonna find her, Syd," he says, voice slow and heavy from the weed.

I want to believe Nick is right. He usually is, but I can't shake the dread and the fear. I can't stop hating myself and I don't understand why. Bending over, I dig my fingers into my forehead and hide behind my dreads.

Nick's hand rests on my shoulder, a heavy comfort. My best friend. I've always thought that Nick was my reward for being stuck with the family that I did—parents who hated me and a sister who was so wonderful even I couldn't help but love her, even though I wanted to hate her. I always looked at everything Mia had and said, "Well, at least I've got Nick." But now? I wish Mia had someone like him. I wish she had a friend that didn't make her run away and drive and get lost.

"What if she's already dead?" I whimper.

Nick pulls me against him, into his bear-body. He's tall and muscular, but kind of heavy, too—which gives him the effect of being husky. He's not cute, he's just average. And sweet. I love him just as he is. He's substantial and normal and *real*. I press my face against his shoulder and I cry.

He buries his hands in my dreads and presses his cheek against my forehead. My head aches, pounds. The weed hasn't helped with the pain or my racing mind. I didn't really think it would.

My words spill out of me in a desperate rush. "Mom won't stop crying. She locked herself in their room and won't let anyone in. Dad's frantic and so...so..."

"Shhh," Nick breathes, his fingers smoothing my hair. "Calm down, Syd. You're going to make yourself sick."

I scoff. Calm down? How can I? But he's right. When I work myself up like this, I usually end up barfing and it's not fair to do that to him.

His fingers wander over my bandaged leg. "What happened?"

Feeling my face heat in shame, I try to pull away, to escape, but he holds me.

"Syd," he urges.

"I-" I start, stop, I don't know how to explain. "I got scared," I confess. "I wasn't sure it was true. I tried to wake myself up."

The expression Nick makes breaks my heart. I never want to see his brows drawn like that, to see his lips pursed just so. I look away from him. "Please don't look at me like that."

He scoots closer. "Sydney," he says, wrapping his hand around my leg, "this is serious."

I shrug only because I don't know what else to do. It's not that big of a deal, it doesn't even hurt that much anymore. The pain in my chest is worse.

His fingers tense on my skin. "Don't shrug like that," he hisses. Then after a moment, he says, "Have you been taking your meds?"

I scowl at him. "Of course I have, you ass. You think I want to be insane?"

He closes his mouth and his jaw flexes a few times before he says, "Do you think about hurting yourself a lot? Think about killing yourself?"

I growl at him. "Oh Jesus, Nick, I'm not having suicidal thoughts!"

"Well," he flounders, "maybe the medicine—"

"It's not my medicine! I'm fine!" I snap.

Looking browbeaten, he chews his lip. "Stabbing yourself is not okay. It's not fine."

I slump my shoulders and lower my chin, defeated. "I know."

His thumb slides over my skin, as if soothing away the wound. "When you do things like this, you know you're not just hurting yourself. I can't stand to see this, Syd. It breaks my heart."

Tears sting my eyes again and I nod. He pulls me close again, kisses my forehead. "Promise me not to do anything like this again. If you're scared, tell me next time. I'm here for you. Always."

"I promise," I whisper into his collar bone. I wish I could just melt into him, let him be the backbone. He always wants to protect me, but he can't. Not from myself.

"And promise you'll tell your therapist about this."

I hesitate for a long moment, trying to weigh the pros and cons of telling Doctor Lebow about it. She'll probably want to change my meds again. I hate when my meds change, it takes me months to adjust—to become the new person they make me. But, if it makes Nick happy...I nod.

"You can do this," he says.

I hold my breath and bite my lip, trying to keep it from trembling because I'm not so sure I can. I'm not so sure I'll win against the demons. Because, even with the meds, it seems they've already beaten me, already damaged me enough that they don't even need to be around for me to cause insanity in my life—to hurt myself and the people around me.

He shifts, pulling me away and grasping my face in his big hands so that he's holding me still with his blue eyes. "You gotta be strong. You gotta have faith in your sister."

I keep holding my breath. Faith. In Mia.

"She's smart and she's strong, right?"

I nod. She's the A student. She's the athlete. She's my perfect sister. She always has a plan, always knows what to do. She always has the answers, always knows what to say to make it okay.

But sometimes, even perfect people need help.

# Fifteen:
# Mia

The rain pounds against the windows, streaking down in rivulets. They're little streams merging into rivers, reflecting the street lights from below so that they send phantom shadows dancing all over my room. Along the cut abs of the Abercrombie models Ti and I cut out of shopping bags and taped on my walls, across the inside out Victoria Secret sweat pants and striped thong underwear on the floor, across John's arm laying in front of me.

Lightning and thunder strike simultaneously, making me jump, and he pulls me closer. "Shhh," his breath is a quiet hiss into my hair. He knows I'm afraid of thunder. That's why he stayed with me tonight, that's how we ended up here in my bed—he was trying to distract me I think, maybe prove that good things happen during thunderstorms. His body curls around me, his skin warm and his strength safe. "I got you."

I close my eyes and smile, pleased beyond comprehension at those words. He does have me. All of me, and I can't think of anything better.

*His hand lifts and traces patterns on my forearm. "What are you thinking about?"*

*I wriggle in his arms, turning myself around in his embrace to face him. More lightning brightens the room, illuminating him. His expression steals all good sense from me and for a moment, I can't find the words.*

*He reaches up and slides a lock of hair behind my ear, traces my jaw, touches my lips, and his eyes meet mine. "You know I love you, right?"*

*I smile at him and break eye contact at the same moment the boom of thunder chases the lightning. I stiffen. He grasps my jaw, angling my face as he leans in to kiss me. Long, deep. He slides his body closer to mine, distracting me, telling me not to focus on what's going on outside because everything that matters is right here in my bedroom.*

*Sighing, I kiss him back, locking my arms around him and letting him roll me onto my back. He breaks away from the kiss, meeting my eyes again.*

*I touch his face. "I love you. More than anything. Forever." And I kiss him again.*

\*\*\*

Thunder booms, making the floor rattle. Frightened, I blink awake. "John?!" I cry, frightened. But something chokes the word back, making me wince. It takes me a moment to remember what's going on, where I am. To realize he's not here to hold me. He never will be. I made him go away.

I close my eyes and suppress the whimper that builds in my chest.

In the deep dark of night, I lay as still as I can because even breathing hurts. Even over the rain, I can hear The Butcher snoring in a room nearby.

Every gasping breath out of him is like nails up my spine.

I'm so exhausted and I wish that I could sleep as peacefully as he apparently can after doing what he did, but I can't—not after what happened today.

I never thought pain like that existed. Acid fire and burning ice, something that ripped and crawled up every nerve ending. The pain hasn't gone away, just turned into something new. A constant beating throb, one that matches my headache. He did nothing to ease the pain he caused, just left me, raw and bleeding. My calf is literally torn to shreds. Even if I could get free, I don't know if I could walk. The whole thing pulsates and aches, bruised where it's not cut because he held it down so hard to keep me from destroying his precious design.

So much blood, so much gore. I thought I was going to die. But he knew how to cut just deep enough, avoiding certain veins. Taking his time. Eventually it was too much and I faded, but I'm awake now. I can see what he did to me in the light of the full moon. Black blood, silver-blue light.

I close my eyes. It burns. Everything burns as if my skin has turned to desert. How long since I've had water? I'm going to die soon. I'll die of blood loss or of dehydration or of shock. Maybe a potent combination of all three. I hope it comes soon. I try to swallow, but my throat is as ragged as my leg. I screamed until I broke. Until my throat exploded and I started sputtering up blood. I don't have a voice now. Nothing to show him my pain.

In a sick way, I kind of like that. He seemed to like it more when I showed him my pain.

Thunder booms again, like the sky is cracking above me. My heart hammers and I stare up at the ceiling, waiting for God to finally pound his fist through the firmament, through the roof, and take me—save me.

93

The lightning shudders strobe-light bright, then winks out.

Stillness. Darkness. Pounding rain. My ragged breathing, like a bent old woman. Stinging tears on my temples, in my hair.

The door creaks open. I try to glance over, but my body is so tired and weak that even moving my eyes is too much. I hold my breath, fearing it's my killer come back to finish the job, but then I realize that he's still snoring.

Is it the ghost?

I'm certain there's some kind of spirit here. The Butcher talked to it, didn't he? And things had moved around on their own, hadn't they? The ghost had stolen The Sisters out of the room. Is it real? Have I been driven mad by fear or perhaps hallucinating on the drug that The Butcher injected me with out on the country road?

Or am I truly insane? Schizophrenia has a genetic component, maybe I'm going crazy like Sydney? I'm not sure if I think that's good or bad.

There's some shuffling about in the room adjoining my death-cell. I hear the distinct sound of a bottle of pills falling onto the floor. The next moment, it comes rattling out of the bathroom and makes a purposeful advance toward the bed. It stops about a yard away and then seems to flop about, as if confused. Finally, it goes still. A moment later, it goes flying across the room and bashes into the wall. It clatters to the floor and stays there.

Next, a package of bandages does the same thing, advancing, flopping, flying. Then ointment, then towels. I watch in confusion as more and more of the bathroom's contents come parading into the room only to dance for a few moments then join the growing heap under the window.

I can't help but grin at the unique rendition of Mickey's "Sorcerer's Apprentice" routine. At least being insane is entertaining. I suppose I should be worried about this, but honestly? I've got worse things to worry about.

Eventually the procession stops and the room is still for a long few minutes. I close my eyes, just wanting it all to end. The exhaustion and pain suck at me, drawing me close to unconsciousness. Something brushes my forehead. My hair...moving across my skin even though there is no wind. I don't have the energy to open my eyes to see what it is. It could be a spider or a cockroach...I don't care. After The Butcher, I've endured worse. It's not a bad touch. It doesn't hurt and it reminds me that there are things that tread softly on this earth, good touches. Like John's.

John.

I let out a long sigh.

God, I'm going to die with bad blood between us. Between me and Ti. I just... Just...

Words come from far away. A male voice, whispering to me. "I'm sorry. I'm not strong enough."

*So am I. Neither am I.*

The pain sucks me down. Drowns me in my own blood.

# Sixteen:
# Corey

Cutter is on track for forgetting that my inmate needs to be tended. He has a tendency to forget, sometimes for days at a time, that the bodies chained to the bed upstairs are humans, not bleeding canvases.

He sits at the kitchen table whistling that same stupid song to himself, sipping strong coffee and reading yesterday's paper. He never gets mail or papers delivered here, that would allow someone to get too close to his broken-down sanctum—more than a hundred acres of farmland covered in wild grass and a muddy, mosquito-infested cow pond. A battered two-story farmhouse with a yawning attic and a creepy basement housing a hell-hound. A lopsided garden shed. A decaying barn filled with rusty old farm equipment, cars, and tractors.

I reach into an open cabinet and shove out a box of oatmeal. It lands on the counter, spilling apple cinnamon packets onto the floor. I scoot one over the cracked tile and leave it meaningfully in the doorway.

Cutter glances up at me. "What? You want me to feed the Little Duck?"

I shove a half-consumed bottled water away from where he left it next to his oil-stained lunch box.

He snaps his paper. "I shouldn't. I should let her suffer after what you did yesterday. You kidnapped my girls."

Growling at him, I shove Nadine out from where I hid her just out of arm's reach under the refrigerator. She comes skidding out, trailing dust bunnies, and hits the opposite counter with a *thunk*.

He puts down the paper and grins at me. "That's better. You cooperate, I'll be nice to your little girlfriend."

I punch him. Just 'cause I want to. But it does nothing. He turns, grabs his half-finished breakfast of eggs and ham, and heads toward the basement door. I keep my distance as he opens it and tosses the plate's contents into the damp, murky beyond. There are no stairs to the basement—most likely to keep Delilah where she belongs—so the eggs and bacon fall through space. Below, I hear Delilah snap something out of the air, her slobbery jaws clacking.

I shiver. Delilah isn't natural. Perhaps she was once a nice little puppy, but years of being locked alone in the dark wet of a basement with only a cistern and whatever Cutter tosses her to eat have turned her into something else. A crazed monster, half starved and living in her own filth, raised to do what Cutter needs of her. Yet, at the same time, I pity her. Usually I like animals, and she's the victim of cruelty. But again, there's nothing I can do for her. Uselessness is the story of my life.

\*\*\*

I trudge after Cutter as he brings a tray of simple food up to my inmate. He puts the food on the hospital table and pushes it over the bed. I watch, concerned, as he unlocks the shackles with a key that he never takes from around his neck, but she doesn't stir.

Is she still alive? I reach out and touch her skin. She's still warm. Too warm. She has a fever. I glance around the floor searching for the aspirin I tried to give her last night. My ability to push things is so limiting. Much as I had good intentions to aid her when I finally found the courage to present myself to her in shame, I couldn't help her. I shove the aspirin until it hits Cutter's boot.

He leans down and picks it up. "Ibuprofen, huh?" He pops the cap and rattles a few into his hand. "I suppose."

He sits on the edge of the bed and gives the inmate a shake. "Wake up, Little Duck, it's time for breakfast."

Stormy blue eyes, made so much more frighteningly bright by the burst blood vessels in each, crack open and swivel toward him. Her throat bobs once and she winces. Poor thing, she's in bad shape.

Cutter pulls her gag out of her mouth. She has a rash and bloodstains across her cheeks, making her look like an even sicker, more twisted version of The Joker.

He cleans her face, gives her some Neosporin and smears some Vaseline on her cracked lips. He wraps her swollen, bloody leg with the same kind of meticulous slowness that he uses when he cuts into flesh.

Cutter is nicer to her than he was with me.

I'm not sure if it's because she's a girl and he thinks she's attractive or if it's because I've still got a goodly number of The Sisters held hostage and he feels he needs to please me.

I don't understand it. Sometimes it's like he cares. Sometimes it's like he wants to be tender and prevent further pain...yet he relishes it the other half of the time. I can't help but wonder if he's bipolar or schizophrenic or what?

When he's done wrapping her wounds, he grabs her under the armpits and props her up. Her body is so limp that her head lolls against her shoulder. She's unshackled now, but she couldn't run if she wanted to. He gives her water and makes her choke down the Ibuprofen, massaging her throat to make her swallow despite the pain. Then he feeds her. Tiny spoonfuls of apple cinnamon oatmeal. But he quickly loses patience with how slowly she manages to swallow it down.

He gives up after half a dozen tries and, setting the bowl on the table, chains her back up and leaves for work.

I sit on the other side of the bed and examine her. "You okay?" It's a dumb question. Of course she's not okay. I just don't know what to say to her. What do you say to someone in her situation if you're someone in my situation? I just want to apologize over and over to her, but that won't do any good. Once is good enough. It's not like she cares anyway.

Groaning to herself, she lifts her chin and stares down at herself. Between the blood and the heat and being tied in one spot for over 24 hours, she could use another bath.

What she really needs is to be free. I look down at her now bandaged leg. The ragged flesh underneath doesn't look good. I'm worried she'll get gangrene or something.

She has lost too much blood...she's too weak. At this rate? She might not live through the next 48 hours...especially if Cutter comes home feeling creative.

What can I do? What helps with blood loss? I don't remember... Sugar? Something with iron? I stare down into her barely touched bowl of oatmeal. It's really thick and glompy now. If I could, I'd take it downstairs, reheat it with more hot water and pop it in the blender. It would be easier for her to drink it. I'll have to somehow get Cutter to do that for her when he gets home. Which means I'll probably have to retrieve another one of The Sisters.

She starts making a strange noise. I glance up, curious. She's trying to talk.

"No," I breathe, sitting forward and putting my hands to her mouth. She goes still, her expression confused. "Don't talk. You'll only make it worse." I lower my hand and put it to her throat, trying to convey what I mean.

Her eyes waver back and forth, searching for something that isn't there for her. She wants help, she's looking for it anywhere she can. Even in me.

I can't stand it.

I pull away. "There is nothing more I can do for you. I'm sorry." I leave her sitting there, staring at where I just was, and retreat out of the room, hiding on the other side of the heavy wooden door.

I stare one way and then the next, the narrow hall offering me nothing but closed doors that lead to confusing pieces of Cutter's past. A woman's room, locked and untouched with layers of dust and grime. A mirror room, but this one for a child, dated, so I always assumed it was his. Cutter's room, dirty and Spartan. The Room behind me. The door to the attic steps. A bare window with spider webs and dead flies littering the sill.

I turn away and go down the stairs, trailing my fingers on the walnut banister, pondering on the shadow spot imprints of where photographs used to hang. I don't bother with the living room that reminds me too much of a fluffy, old middle-income sitcom or the kitchen that looks like it belongs in an old lake house.

*** 

Out in my garden, I dig my fingers into the soil and leave them there. I need the rasp of dusty earth on my palms, need the cool damp on my fingers beneath. Contact. Something I hardly ever have. I can touch earth. I can touch water. I can touch plants and animals. That's what I'm allowed to touch. Other humans? Much as I can feel them, I'm nothing but a phantom to them

I pull one hand out of the dirt and touch my face. I can feel me. I can still breathe, my heart still beats, and I still sweat. I feel with my skin and my heart. Doesn't that mean something?

I look up and survey my playground. A half acre of fenced in beauty. The bees travel, fat and heavy, from drooping lily trumpet to fragrant rose to bursting daisy. I crawl into the shade of the sunflowers lined against the fence and drape an arm over my eyes. The sun is warm and the air is still and cloying. Last night's rain has made it humid and today's hot sun has already dried everything until it cracked. I wish for more rain, for a torrential downpour that will drown everything like Noah's flood. Everything could use a good cleansing. Myself especially.

# Seventeen:
# Sydney

I lift another flier and smash the stapler against it, taking out my frustration. Nick shifts beside me, his ADHD never did make him the most focused person, but he's been good about not complaining about helping me with this. He trails me to another one of the lampposts sticking out of the boardwalk.

As he hands me another flier, I try not to read it, try not to look at my sister's face as I canvas it over a posting for someone looking for a roommate from two months ago.

"I'm hot," he says. "I'm gonna get something to drink. You want something?"

I glance over my shoulder and stare at him. He's got a sunburn. We've been out since this morning. I probably have one, too. He does look hot; hot, sweaty, miserable. He's doing this for me. For me and for Mia.

I look down at my red Converses. "Yeah. We should take a break, I guess."

His fingers find my free hand and he squeezes it. "Come on."

Nick leads me a little farther down the boardwalk, to where there are some picnic tables set up beside the burger stand. He steers me toward an empty one near the railing so that I look out over the beach while sitting under the shade of an umbrella. I plop down and, after a moment, I feel his fingers pry the stapler out of mine. I'm dimly aware of him placing it on top of the stack of fliers before his hands return to pull my backpack off of my shoulders. He's too good to me, taking care of me when I should be taking care of myself. I need to snap the hell out of this stupor, but I can't seem to move my arms.

Nick leans close and presses his lips against my forehead. Too hot in the summer sun, but good. His hands squeeze my shoulders. "I'll be back in a couple of minutes."

I nod, if only to let him know that I know he's there with me and I appreciate him.

I listen to his flip flops disappear into the press of bodies around us and stare out over the railing. It's a blue sky, bright sun day. Which means everyone and their cousin Vinny is at the beach.

Down there, the press of bare-skin bodies is thick, just like the press of bodies milling around behind me. Eating their fried food, drinking their slushies, playing games for cheap prizes, weaving in and out of shops and arcades and photo booths. I can hear the screams of the kids at the amusement and water park down at the next pier.

I bet they don't know about Mia. I bet they don't care. I didn't. Not until it was my own sister whose face was staring back at me from the missing person flier. It makes me hate them. But it makes me hate myself even more.

A familiar, tittering laugh from behind me catches my attention. Straightening, I turn around and scan the crowd.

And there she is. Tiana. And she's smiling and laughing, her arm intertwined in Will's. Both without a goddamned care in the world. They stop at the burger stand and flirt with each other as they talk about the menu.

My hearing seems to narrow in on that grating, stupid voice. My eyes on that careless, serpent smile. My heart speeds up and my blood turns to acid. I see red.

Before I know what I'm doing, I'm on my feet and running at Tiana. I sack her—making us both tumble to the dry, sandy wood. She twists underneath me, confused and trying to get up, but I don't let her. I hit her. Fist to fat cheek. And the noise her head makes when it smacks against the wood makes me feel good. So I do it again.

Someone yells my name.

And again. Back forth, back forth, like a rhythm of justice being pounded into her flesh.

Until strong hands grab me and drag me off. "What the hell is wrong with you?!"

I know that voice, too, but I don't respond to it. Instead, I wriggle in his grasp, kicking at the air, trying to get to my target. "Stupid slut!" I scream. The voice doesn't sound like mine. But it feels good. More words come out, things I've never said before, and they drive her backward in a bloody-nosed, cow-eyed crab-walk.

I want to go after her. I want to beat every word into her face until she's branded with them—Scarlet Letter style.

Will pulls her to her feet. She stares at me, her giant brown eyes tear and her dumb little mouth begins to snivel.

She looks so clueless, so stupidly innocent. What's she confused for? She knows she's a traitor, she knows what she's done.

"Calm down!" The voice holding me shakes his words into me.

I continue squirming, leaning toward her so she can see that I'm an avenging angel and she will not escape me. "It's your fault, you dumb bitch! It's all your fault!"

The person holding me drags me against him, shackles me against his chest with strong arms. It's then that I recognize him—by smell of all things. Chlorine and Axe, Mia used to come home smelling like this. John. The other half of Mia. And just like that, I start sobbing, but I don't give up. I claw at the air, trying to get to Tiana. "I'm gonna kill her! I hate her!"

So much hate. So much heat. Rabbit fast heart, lion desires. I could explode.

Tiana isn't even looking at me anymore. She's whimpering into Will's chest and he's fawning over her, his eyes glancing darkly in my direction.

"Get her out of here, would you?" John barks.

Will drags Tiana away, but I don't stop struggling. I'll find her, no matter what. I will make her pay.

"What's going on?" Nick's voice, shrill with concern, cuts through the startled voices around me, through the blood rushing in my ears and my snarling remarks.

Suddenly ashamed of myself, I bury my face in John's chest and hide from Nick. He wouldn't like me like this. This is not the girl he loves. This is an insane girl, an uncontrolled girl. A girl who has to make confessions to her therapist and get her meds changed.

John's grasp on me loosens, his restraint becoming a hug. I always did like John. I always thought Mia was an idiot for leaving him.

"I don't know," John's saying, voice settled but confused. "First I'm waiting on customers and the next thing I know, Syd's flying like a bat out of hell and beating them up." His hand grips my shoulder. "What's wrong with you?"

I shake my head against his shoulder, still sobbing and hiccupping. "You-you don't understand."

He sighs and his muscles ease a little around me. "What don't I understand?"

See? This is why I like John. He's wicked patient and he's always seen me and talked to me. I sob into his neck, unwilling to turn around and face Nick's disappointment. "It's-it's her fault. It's all her fault," I whimper.

Another sigh from John. "Come on."

He drags me back to the picnic area and plops me at a new table. I can sense Nick perching on my other side, can feel his anxious eyes on me. John must sense Nick's needs because his body dissolves only to be replaced by Nick's. Nick's arm slips across my shoulder and he's my big teddy bear again. I twine my arms around him and hide against the world. "I'm sorry," I whisper, trying to ignore how his hand is examining my leg, which I've reopened and caused to bleed again in my frenzy. "I don't know what came over me."

Nick's hand pats my lower back, rough palm against the bare skin exposed by my reaching arms. "I do."

"Well, would you care to enlighten me, please?" John says.

I finally look up and glance over my shoulder.
John's wearing a white collared shirt, a stained apron, and one of those stupid hats they wear at the burger joint. I blink at him, confused, until I remember Mia telling me that working at the burger joint is his summer job this year.

I meet John's expectant hazel eyes. They look so warm in the summer sun. And then it occurs to me that John doesn't know about Mia yet. 'Cause if he did, he wouldn't be here. He wouldn't be able to carry on, flipping burgers and lining fry baskets, like nothing happened. Mia is John's world. Just like Nick is my world.

And I can't be the one to destroy his world like some bad version of Godzilla. Can I? He has a right to know. He'll hate me for not saying anything when he does eventually find out. The police will get to questioning him, eventually. And Dad will only be able to keep this out of the media for so long.

Before I make up my mind, fate decides for me. A hot gust of air tears at the stack of fliers sitting on the table next to us, knocking the stapler to the side and blowing them out and around us.

John, ever helpful, ever a dumb little Boy Scout, jumps up and runs after them. He catches three before my sister's smile traps his eyes, freezing him mid-grab like some kind of awkward still-life statue in the middle of the boardwalk.

The people move around him, their feet shuffling my sister's face into the grit, shoving her to the side with the rest of the trash. They move like ants around John. So alive, so carefree. But not John. John is a watch winding down, his limbs losing strength and coming to rest, his head drooping. The life going out of his eyes, his breath becoming still. John is dead.

Nick sees it, too, because he draws me closer and tucks me against him, his chin coming to rest on my head. A reassurance that we are both still there for each other, because neither of us ever wants to go through what John is now going through—to lose the one who means everything. Again. In a worse way than being broken up with.

But suddenly, John's head snaps up and the world starts ticking again. I stare at him, amazed by the fire in his eyes. Jaw set, he storms toward me and shoves the flier in my face. "What is this?"

I open my mouth, but the words stick, so I try sinking into Nick instead. As if I could hide from the intensity in John's expression.

Nick speaks for me. "It's true, man. She's been missing since Friday night."

John's chest is heaving. He snatches the paper back and grasps it in both hands, staring hard at it. "Why didn't anyone tell me? What happened?" It looks like he's asking Mia's picture that, not me or Nick. But Mia's demure smile will tell him nothing.

I sit up, abandoning Nick's shelter and forcing myself to have a back bone. "She went for a drive after she left Ti's party. They found her abandoned car last night. That's when Dad filed the missing person's report."

"Why didn't you tell me?"

I shrug. I should have. I know I should have. Next to me and my parents, John and Tiana love her most. They should have both been told. They shouldn't have found out like this. But I guess since Tiana betrayed Mia and Mia apparently no longer loves John, I didn't think it mattered. It does, though. I come up with a lame excuse. "We haven't told many people yet, Dad didn't want it to hit the news."

"But-" he holds up the flier.

I bite my lip. "They don't know I'm doing this." Dad will kill me when the reporters start showing up, but...I can't just sit for another day and do nothing. I can't. The helplessness is suffocating me.

John's fists tighten on the paper and his voice shakes as he asks, "Are there any leads?"

I shake my head.

He seems angered by this. "Well, what are the police doing? Haven't they questioned everyone that was at the party?"

I shake my head. "She went missing in upstate New York, John. No one at the party had anything to do with it."

He blinks. "What? What the hell was she doing up there?"

I shrug, not wanting to tell him about Will. That would only hurt John more, so I say, "She had a fight with Tiana and went for a drive to blow off some steam."

Realization dawns in his handsome features and he glances in the direction Will and Tiana slunk off in. "Hence why it's Ti's fault?"

I give a stiff nod.

His hand lifts and he shoves it through his hair, knocking his stupid burger joint hat to the boardwalk. "Damn it. I knew something was wrong when I saw her leave the party." He closes his eyes and tilts his head to the side, his face looking like he's enduring something painful. "I should have gone after her."

I shake my head. Dealing with John was probably the last thing Mia wanted to do after losing her chances with Will. "Don't you dare blame yourself, John. It wouldn't have helped. You know how stubborn she is. She would have just blown up at you and then drove away anyway."

He lowers his chin, his jaw muscles tightening. For a long moment, he's quiet—staring hard at where a couple of fliers are pasted against the employee door of the burger joint. Then he looks up and pegs me with those eyes of his. "I want to help."

# Eighteen:
# Mia

The day is a haze where minutes become hours and asleep and awake turn into the same repeating dream-nightmare. I'm back in a safe place, watching TV with Ti, dancing with John on the boardwalk, sitting on the floor painting my nails with my sister, then all of a sudden there's a wicked face and a savage knife cutting into me. Slicing me open, making me bleed, making me beg and scream, collapsing the movie screens all around me until there's only black and fun house mirrors stretching me to nothing.

The sun moves across the floor again and again, the shadow beckoning and teasing—close and far, close and far.

I sink further. My body drooping, my mind sucking inward. Escaping. Going so deep that even movement is too far away and monumental a request. Blocks of stone being knocked one by one into the well until it levels, sinks, fills up, becomes dry and forgotten.

I'm beyond the throbbing pain and ache.

I close my eyes, willing the curtains to stop waltzing in the sun.

Stop.
Stop it.
Make it go away.

\*\*\*

*"I can go higher than you!"*

*"No you can't!" I pump my legs harder, faster. My body swings back and forth, fighting gravity, flirting with the earth and the sky. My feet touch the sun, skim in the dirt. My heart is pounding, my smile could crack my face.*

*I hear Ti laughing. "I'm winning!"*

*"No! No way!" I scream.*

*But it's the truth. She is winning. She always did win. Why couldn't I just let her win? Why?*

*Unwilling to let her best me, I yank my arms inward and let my butt slide off the swing as I fly at the sun. I fly. Air, air, air, then boom, in the dirt. I feel the sting of the grit in my hands and my knee.*

*"Show off!" she yells.*

*I smile in triumph. She never did have the balls to jump after me. But then pain makes me look down. Blood...*

*Laughing laugh. Horrible Butcher face with his knife. He slashes at me, a pressurized sting that drags and lingers. The heat oozes up, spills over. Lava. I scream and I run, but I'm only going in circles and every time I rotate around, he cuts me deeper, harder.*

\*\*\*

Cool whisper touch rouses me. A breeze in the stillness, over leg, over arm, over cheek. I lean into it, needing the centering balm of it to find the will to open my eyes again.

Someone is sitting beside me. A boy. "You're awake."

Heavy lidded, I blink with the uncertainty of a drug-stupor. Is he real? An angel? Please, God, let him be the angel of death. *Take me away.*

His grey eyes dart toward the nightstand. "I brought you a gift."

I follow his gesture. There's a pile of dirt in the center, like a little mountain. And springing from the very top is a single white daisy. Strong and alive, the center a sweet bright yellow. For some reason, it reminds me of Ti and my heart sinks further. Ti. My sweet Ti. I miss her. Even if she betrayed me. Had she loved Will, too? I don't know. I never asked. Had we been in love with the same boy for forever? It seems silly now, my tears and anger. She can win. She can have Will. I just want to hug her now.

More tugging at my heart. And I want to hug John. God, I miss him. I want him here. I want him to hold my hand and be the brave one. I never felt more safe and secure than when I was with him. I want to say I'm sorry and that, even though I left him, I never broke my promise of loving him forever.

And poor Sydney. Why was I ever so mean to her? Isn't it bad enough that our parents favored me? I had to rub it in as well? What kind of person am I?

I've hurt all the people I love. Maybe I deserve this? Maybe this is my Karmic reckoning...

The boy sitting in front of me reaches out and brushes his fingers over my forehead, easing sweaty locks away from fevered skin. Dark brows crimp down over warm eyes. "Your fever is getting worse."

I close my eyes and let myself sink again. His raspy voice does that, makes my insides settle like a cat melting on a hot hearth. Something about it is familiar. Like I've heard it before. I just want to sleep...

No. There's someone here. Someone who can help me. I force my eyes open and try to sit up—to meet his gaze.

"H-h-hel—" I cough and it's like a firebrand being shoved up my throat. Eyes rolling into my head with pain, I collapse back again.

"Shhh," he breathes, his body inching closer to mine. "You're sick. You need rest."

What I need is to be uncuffed and taken to a hospital. I open my eyes again, desperate to convey this to him. Can't he see I need help? Or is he in league with my captor?

As if sensing my thoughts, he says, "God, I wish I could help you."

I wrinkle my forehead. *Why can't you?* I glance down, trying to see if he is chained and bound like I am. He doesn't look it. He looks tall and strong. He could punch Cutter. He could carry me down the stairs, drive me to the hospital.

"I've tried to stop him, tried to get you out, but..." He lifts his hand and places it against my wrist, two of his fingers pressing into my palm and the others circling my wrist. I force myself to turn my head and see. His hand is inside of the cuff or, rather, the cuff is inside his hand.

*Oh.* I lean my head back against the headboard. This is it. This is the end. I'm seeing stuff. More hallucinations. From the fever? Maybe from shock? Did I make him up? To give me comfort in my final hours of death?

Shouldn't he look like someone I know? Someone I want to see? John? Not some stranger...not a boy I don't associate with love and comfort.

Why isn't insanity comforting? Shouldn't it be comforting?

He speaks. "I can't do much," he admits, voice acidic and glum. His eyes flash up, determined and strong. "I want to. I swear it, I do." He looks so fierce and earnest. He's tall and solid and muscular. He could kill Cutter if he'd just take up one of those knives and fight him. I don't understand.

He looks away, lowering his head and shoving big hands into shaggy black curls. He's Greek or Italian, I think, though he has the kind of bone structure in his face that makes me think he might be English, too. His face is familiar, yet not. Perhaps I have seen him before...we don't hallucinate or dream people we've never seen before, right?

And then it hits me. I *have* seen this guy's face before. On the internet. Geez, those sad stories that people circulate around Facebook really are true. "Corey," I croak, my voice nearly a whisper.

His head snaps up and he gives me an uneasy expression. "You-you can see me?"

For a long moment, I just stare at him, uncertain if he's joking.

He scoots closer and leans in, so close we're almost nose to nose. "Can you hear me?"

I give him a calculating look. Great. He's crazier than the guy with the knives. Maybe the Cheshire Cat had it right when he told Alice that everyone was mad. Even so, I nod.

A breath escapes him and he smiles, huge and white. He then launches into a fast-paced, one-sided conversation with himself. "Shit. This is great! Wait, wait." He touches his chin in thought. "This is probably not great. If you can see me that must mean something is different. Something is weird, like you're closer to death or something... Yeah, that's probably not good. But what should I do about it? I don't know. What can I do?"

I rattle my chains, trying to get his attention. When he looks up, startled, I sigh and give him an annoyed look. I don't like being talked about like I'm not here. And he's freaking me out, talking to himself like this and acting like it's some kind of miracle that I acknowledge his existence.

Of course he's here, it makes perfect sense. We are in the house of a kidnapper, after all. Why wouldn't someone who has been missing for almost a year be here, too?

He lowers his hand. "I'm sorry. That was rude. I shouldn't be rude to you. I'm just..." he searches for the right word, "out of practice, I guess."

I'm not entirely sure this guy ever *was* in practice.

"So," he continues, voice obviously still excited, "how do you know my name?"

Holy cow. I can't believe I found him! Or did he find me? It doesn't matter. This guy has been missing since last winter. He was the top news story for months because he went missing on a school trip and his dad— some kind of internet mogul—went nuts conducting a national search. What's he doing? Shouldn't he be tied up? Shouldn't he, if he has managed to escape his chains, be running? Does he have Stockholm Syndrome or something? I want to ask all of this, but it hurt just to say his name.

He saves me by looking down at his hands and answering himself. "That's a stupid question," he reflects then gives me a curious expression. "The news?"

I nod.

He purses his lips. "Are my mom and dad okay?"

I give him a puzzled look. How should I know that? I'm not the family therapist.

All I know is that everyone thought he'd been kidnapped for ransom. His father was offering a friggin' fortune for his safe return but no one ever came forward. That's probably what will happen with me and my dad... Eventually, Corey faded from the news and we all went back to caring more about the Kardashians. I'm sure I'll fade, too.

Corey reaches out toward me. I flinch away from him at first because I'm still unsure if he's friend or foe. He goes still, hand outstretched. "I'm not gonna hurt you." He continues reaching forward.

I let him touch me, only because I'm bound and don't really have a choice. And once his fingers dance along the skin of my neck, I'm glad I did. I need another human's touch. I need to be reminded again that good touch is possible. His fingers fumble with my Tiffany necklace, shoving it around until it bumps up against my clavicle. He squints at it and for a moment, I'm not sure what he's doing.

"Mia," he breathes, his breath tickling my neck. "Is that your name?"

I nod and wriggle away from him. He's too close, like he forgot how to function with other people. Or was he always like this? Either way, he has no right to my personal space. Especially now when I'm bound, vulnerable, and hurt; and he still hasn't released me. Plus, I don't like him touching my necklace. John gave it to me as a birthday present.

He seems okay with my need for space because he straightens and looks away from me. "I wonder if Cutter knows our names," he says. "Do you think he cares?"

*Cutter?* Does he mean the guy with the knives?

"He never calls me by my name. Even after all this time. Doesn't call you by yours either."

I narrow an eye at him, confused by the melancholy look in his eye. It's like it actually bothers him that this Cutter guy doesn't know his name.

He draws his knees up and shackles his arms around his legs, as if hugging himself, and looks out over the room. "I still can't figure him out. Even after all this time."

Yup, Stockholm Syndrome for sure.

I stare at him, still uncertain. He's being nice now, but what the hell is he doing here? And why am I still locked up? I rattle my chain again, trying to get his attention. He glances up at me and I try to convey the urgency of needing his help.

He gives me such sad eyes. So deep and forlorn. He stands. "I can't, Mia."

I shake my head. I don't want to hear that. I want to get out. I rattle my chains again, desperate. *Don't be afraid of what Cutter will do, just let me go and we can both run away. Be free.* I tell him all of this with my eyes. My hope is a stubborn thing, telling me that, if only I can win Corey's trust, I can get him to set me free.

Corey draws a deep breath and shoves his hand into his hair again. His eyes begin roving all over the room, as if searching for something. But we're interrupted by the door opening downstairs.

# Nineteen:
# Corey

I straighten and glance at Mia. Her expression has closed down to the very basic of primal fear. Cutter is home.

Swallowing hard, I motion for her to keep quiet and slide from the room. As I come downstairs, I see that Cutter has again visited the liquor store and didn't wait to get home for me to destroy the habit. The bottle of vodka is half gone and he's weaving around the kitchen, preparing for dinner. Eggs. He always eats eggs.

I cross my arms and lean against the doorjamb. "Oh, real classy."

He wobbles in place as he cracks eggs in the pan.

"You've got a sick girl upstairs. You need to take care of her." Nothing. I don't know why I bother. I advance on him, grabbing his arm and shoving the pan across the stove and out from under him. "Hey!"

He goes still and blinks. The egg he just cracked— one handed—slides out of the shell and hisses as it plops onto the electric burner.

He stares down at it, like he doesn't quite understand what's going on. I stare at him, hoping that for once, he's listening to me.

Next thing I know, he's screaming and there's a pan of greasy eggs flying at my head. I duck on impulse and it flies across the room. Instinct has me leaping at his stomach in an effort to get him to the floor, but that doesn't really work. I just summersault across the cracked linoleum tiles like a *Karate Kid* flunkey. I hit the screen door with an *oomph* and crumple into a heap.

"Idiots! Morons! Mother fuckers said I was nothing! Nothing! God damn it!"

It takes me a disoriented moment to register that Cutter must have come home angry about something that happened at work and is now more than a little pissed off that I ruined his snack time. He's having a tantrum, knocking down chairs and throwing things and cussing up a storm. Next thing I know, he's hauling ass up the stairs, still howling.

"I'll show you! I'm better than you!"

I scramble to my feet, my shoes squeaking against the tile, and run after him. By the time I make it into The Room, he's already pounding his meaty fist into Mia's stomach.

"Stupid whore! Stupid cunt!" he bellows.

Her mouth and eyes are gaping as she moans, trying to beg mercy; her hands are wide claws and straining against the chains. She's thrashing and squirming. She wants to ball up and cover herself, but she can't.

It makes my blood explode hot and hard through my veins. With a wild howl, I run at him again, intent on tackling him, but I just fly head over heels, tumbling onto Mia.

I throw myself over her, trying to cover her shaking body with mine. "No! Stop it!" I scream. Her heart beats mouse-scared beneath mine and her breath is a mewling rasp against my neck.

"I'll show you!" His hand finds its way through my skull, through my brain. I hear flesh meeting flesh and her body slams sideways underneath mine. And then she's still. For a moment, I'm terrified that she's dead.

"I'll show you! Dumb bitch!" He hits her twice more, each time losing more steam until he staggers backward and blinks down at us—me breathing like I've run a marathon and Mia broken and beaten unconscious beneath me. I feel my own terror and hatred on my face. Know it is reflected in his eyes. I've never thought myself capable of murder. But I know, in this moment, I would do worse things to Cutter if I were physically able. I would make him suffer and bleed and I would enjoy it. Because he'd deserve every moment of it.

Suddenly, Cutter begins shaking like a withdrawing junkie. He balls his fists again, advances forward and plants his foot against the side of the bed. He shoves it hard, making it scrape and rattle across the room until it hits the wall. I brace myself over Mia, as if somehow I could do anything. And then, just like that, Cutter backpedals into the far wall, buries his face in his hands, and begins bawling.

# Twenty:
# Sydney

My fork scrapes against my plate as I sit with John at our otherwise empty dining room table. Mom's still shut in my parents' room. Dad says he's not hungry and is just sitting in the living room, staring out the window. I'm not hungry either, but I know I need to eat. I shove my noodles into my gravy.

John made dinner. Nothing fancy, just bland chicken, noodles, and frozen green beans, but it's better than the PB&J I would have made myself if it were just me.

"Where did they say the car was, exactly?"

I try to focus—to find words. John's full of questions, he's the only one with his head screwed on tight. I've never seen him this intense, not even at swim meets. "I don't know."

"Well," he says into his own untouched plate, "we'll have to find out. We can go looking on our own."

I grip the edge of my shorts, tugging at the frayed edges. "What if...what if what we find is..." I can't even say the words. What if she's dead? What if we find her body laying on the side of the road somewhere?

John's deep growl draws my eyes. "That's not gonna happen, Syd. She's alive, I know she is."

I nod, though I don't feel as certain. "I-I need to go to bed." I push away from the table and head toward the stairs. For whatever reason, I stop in the doorway and glance back at John. He's staring fixedly at the wall, but his fists are balled under the table and his broad shoulders are tense. He's chewing his lip. I've never seen him do that before. I glance at the stairs and back at him. "Why don't you sleep in her room tonight?"

John lifts his chin and stares at me wide eyed.

I shrug. "I don't think my parents would notice and...I think she'd like it. She never stopped loving you. You know that, right?"

John looks down again, his shoulders caving inward. "I know." His voice is tight.

So hard, so determined. He loves my sister so much. I drift back into the dining room and lace my fingers under his elbow. He gets up without prompting and lets me lead him to Mia's room.

For a long time, he stands in the doorway staring at what must have once felt like a second home to him. He was here so often. Two years of dating my sister. There must be so many memories, so many ghosts hiding behind the dark piles of her clothes. I know there are for me.

Over the past few days I've just sat in there, remembering late night conversations, heated arguments, laughter, smelling my sister and thinking about what she did in here when her secret temple doors were closed against the world.

The memories are so vivid that it's like she's not gone. I've questioned my sanity over and over, but as promised to Nick, I haven't tested myself again.

Now, it's John's turn to feel her ghost. I reach out and grasp the door handle, drawing the door between him and me, closing him in with the phantom of my sister.

I'm not even to my own door before his sob and the sound of his knees hitting the floor freeze me in my steps. I snap myself out of it, forcing myself not to listen as John totally loses it, and rush into my own room.

I close my own door, shutting out the noise and sink to the floor.

I cry, too, not hard painful sobs, but quiet tears of despair.

When Nick appears, bundling his big body through my open window, he goes still at the sight of me sitting with my legs drawn close in the darkness. I hold my arms out for him and he comes, lifting me up and carrying me to my bed, wrapping me in his arms and laying with me until sleep comes.

No words. There doesn't have to be. Not when you love someone. And that's the only thing I know to be true despite insanity.

# Twenty-One:
# Corey

I stay with Mia. I stay lying right beside her because I'm afraid of leaving her side. Every time I leave her, he hurts her. Sooner or later, she's going to die. I'm terrified of it and I'm terrified for her. Besides him beating her outsides, I'm scared she's becoming too dehydrated. She's not even sweating any more. It's too hot right now. The summer is too much. He took me in winter and I suffered differently than she did. But Cutter had to keep the heat up in the house or risk freezing to death.

Now? He just turns the air conditioner in his room on and lets the rest of the house swelter in hundred degree weather.

I touch her forehead. She's too hot with fever. Her breathing is thready and fast. When I lower my head to her chest, her heart is like a hummingbird batting its wings against my cheek.

"Am I...gonna die?" she whispers. Her voice is a rasp because there is no voice, only air.

"Shhh," I breathe, touching her cracked, tacky lips.

She tries to swallow and I can actually hear the sound of the inside of her throat rubbing against itself. Her blue eyes peer out from bloodshot whites framed by double black eyes. All over again, I want to get my hands on Cutter, I want to beat his face in. No one should hurt someone this small and fragile looking.

She closes her eyes and winces. "Hurts...to breathe."

"I know." I'm willing to bet he probably broke a few ribs. I hope that's all he broke. What if she has internal bleeding? Or a collapsed lung or something?

I shake my head, hating the thought. Closing my eyes, I bury my face in my hands. "This is all my fault. I'm so useless."

I hear her try and swallow again. "Corey—"

I take a shaking breath and try to look brave, to try and be stability for her instability and strength for her weakness. She doesn't need my pity party. It won't do any good for either of us. "Yeah?"

She stares at me long and hard for a really long minute. "Can't...free me?"

I shake my head.

"You...real?"

I squint at her, uncertain how to respond. Am I real? Not in the sense she's asking.

Finally, with a glum sort of finality in her voice, she says, "Ghost?"

I don't react at first. And even when I can—when I can deal with the harsh external reality of it—all I can do is sit up and nod.

# Twenty-Two:
# Mia

I stare at the ghost of Corey Rossi for a long time. I call him ghost because that's what Sydney used to call her hallucinations, those things that she believed—with her whole heart—were real. Corey doesn't seem like a ghost. I can feel him and I can see him and I can hear him. He's warm and breathes like a human. But then, he fell right through Cutter...

I'd seen him trying to stop Cutter from beating me...and he'd fallen right though him. Just like a figment of one's imagination should.

That doesn't make sense because he landed on top of me and he had a body and he had weight. But then Cutter punched right through his body.

He's not real. He's not really a ghost. He's only here because I made him be. A kindred spirit, another lost person who will not be found. He's solid in some ways because I need him to be.

But when it comes to actually freeing me, he can't because that's where the line between reality and imagination is drawn. Imagination cannot impact your external world.

The bottle of pills sitting on the hospital table draw my eye. They had come out of the other room and then the next day, Cutter had given them to me. He didn't go to the other room to get them. And what about the knives? They moved, Cutter's reaction to their movement hadn't been a hallucination...had it?

Things don't make sense.

But then, I can't think straight, can I? I'm sick. It's too hard, even to think.

I can't feel my arms and legs.

What does that mean?

I close my eyes. I don't want to think about it. I don't want to listen to my body telling me I'm dying. I want to be grounded in non-truth. In a fantasy. Maybe that's why I imagined Corey up. "Story," I whisper. My throat feels like fire. Everything feels like dry fire. At least, the parts that I can still feel.

The bed shifts as he looks down at me. "You want me to tell you a story?"

I nod, though I'm not sure if I even move. It feels too heavy and dizzy-making. I squeeze my eyes shut in pain.

Corey reaches out and loops a strand of my hair behind my ear. His touch is gentle, but even that hurts on my bruised, swollen face.

"Okay," he breathes.

But he doesn't continue. I open my eyes, confused. He's staring at me. As if realizing it, he looks away and begins to speak, "When I was alive, I had a crush on this girl, Ashley..."

I close my eyes and listen to Corey's low voice drag me deep and under, into the warm hearth-place. I imagine myself as a child sprawled on a huge bearskin rug—without a care or a pain—and I listen to his story.

He tells me about Ashley. His breaths are a lattice-work of words that build a person bone to bone and then paint skin in delicate strokes. He creates a girl who I want to love just because his voice-poetry makes her beautiful. Her gentle smile lights the room like Victorian floor lamps. Her clean, innocent scent is a zephyr over a cotton-clad hill. The way she moves when she walks is a waltz in tasteful stilettos. Her laugh rises like bubbles and thrills like circus music.

His memory of her keeps her real in a way that he is not; his secret, reverent love gives her a heartbeat. My crazy mind does the rest.

She is a coiffed, emerald-clad, mahogany-haired princess at a Labyrinth-like ball. I follow her between the swirling bodies, desperate to hold her hand, desperate to know her beyond the high school façade of quiet, bookish girl who has never looked at me despite the fact that she should—everyone sees me. She does not. She defies logic and I'm falling deeper and deeper into a white-rabbit slumber, a slumber where my own dreams and my own prince are waiting for me.

Not the boy with the lip ring, but the one with the strong arms and intense eyes. The prince I know and love and hate myself for hurting. The one that I'll never be able to say sorry to or reclaim my love for. Because I'm going to be dead soon. I know that. But, when I die, I want to be like Corey Rossi. I want to be a ghost and I want to go be with John forever.

\*\*\*

When I wake up, Corey is still beside me. He seems to be sleeping as well, but when I shift, he's instantly alert.

I smile at him, though I'm drowsy and heavy-lidded. I don't know if this is sleep or awake anymore. I don't know if I'm dead yet and my spirit self has become interred with Corey. "Fake."

He smiles back, his expression sad. "I miss sleep," he admits. "I miss dreaming. Being awake all the time is lonely."

My fingers ache to touch his face, to let him know he's not alone. As if sensing my thoughts, he looks back down at me. "It's nice to have someone to talk to...I mean, I talk to Cutter all the time. But he doesn't like to talk back." I don't miss the irony in his tone.

I force the painful words out. My tongue feels so fat and heavy, a slimy slug. "What...happened?"

He shrugs. "My story isn't all that different than yours, really. I was on a school trip."

I nod, vaguely remembering the news reporting that Corey was on a school trip in New York City when he went missing.

"I was," he pauses, looking for the right words, "distracted, I guess. Cutter came up from behind me and knocked me out, must have dragged me to his van, brought me here." His slate eyes lift and rove around the room, taking it in. "Tied me up here—just like you." He looks down at his hands and says, "I'm sure you can fill in the blanks from there."

"Yeah," I croak. Neither of us want to talk about something that is already so real. If my imagined Corey is anything like me, Cutter would have introduced him to The Sisters and they would have tasted of his flesh like they have of mine. He would know the same pain and thirst and hunger and fear that I know this very moment. He wouldn't have had a compassionate imaginary ghost to help him through it like I do.

He would have died, hurt and scared and alone. And that's why he's here, so I don't have to die like that.

For a long moment, there is an uncomfortable silence and I don't think Corey's going to tell me anything else. Finally, he says, "It took me about two weeks to die. At least, I think it was that much. You kind of lose track after..." He lifts his hands and rubs them over his face. When he looks at me again, there are tears in his eyes. Ghost tears, but who's to say dead people can't feel pain and terror just as keenly as we do? And the laws of nature can bend when you're crazy. "When death came," he breathes, "I was so happy." He shakes his head, dark curls brushing his high forehead. "I thought—finally. Finally, I'm done. He can't hurt me anymore."

His voice is choked and emotional. I wish I could touch him, reassure him and comfort him like he has done for me countless times since I've arrived here...but I can't. I'm still bound and that just makes it all the more painful. Heart-pain to go along with all the other physical pains that Cutter has sewn into my flesh. A pain that makes me see my own fear, makes me see my own wishes. Because he's only echoing what I want.

He bites a trembling lip and smiles bitterly, his face spasming in a way that shows he's barely holding it together. "But then I woke up..." His voice squeaks, forcing him to take a deep breath and close his eyes. The tears that have been balancing on his eyelids finally escape. One lone tear for each eye. They break my heart. "I was still here."

And there it is. An expression of the true fear. I bite my own lip, making it bleed. What if I end up living this nightmare forever? What if I don't die? Or what if I die and somehow end up staying here?

My soul trapped here, tethered by my need to fulfill everything I ache for—to love John, to reconcile with Ti, to hold my sister's hands when the nightmares come to assault her.

Would I be able to do that? Or would I be shackled to these four walls, screaming and making the floorboards shake with my frustration?

What would be worse? To go or to stay?

I don't know.

# Twenty-Three:
# Corey

Cutter hovers in the doorway, eyes blurry and mouth thin. I sit between him and a sleeping Mia, glaring back at him, daring him to try anything.

"A little early," I say at him, voice as menacing as I can make it.

His eyes rove over Mia, stopping at her bruised and broken face. He closes his eyes and shakes his head.

Unbelievable. A scoff escapes my lips. "Are you actually ashamed of yourself?"

I'm not met with a reply. He simply turns away and goes downstairs. A moment later, I can hear him cleaning up his mess from last night. I hate that man. I hate him with every fiber of my non-existent being.

I hate him even more because sometimes, like now, I feel almost sorry for him. And I almost feel like it would be humane for him to die in the gruesome ways I imagine for him.

As if those wouldn't be horrible experiences for him at all. I half imagine he'd laugh with relief through them.

I shiver as I sit in the already hot Room.

\*\*\*

I go to *Them*. I go to *Them* because I need help. Mia is going to die and Cutter needs to be stopped.

So, I walk through the tall grass and undergrowth. I pass where the fields have grown over in neglect. Underbrush and young trees that shield a broken past. I go to the place where they hide—as far away from him as they can get.

As I approach, I see them gathering—eyes peering through broken smoke-glass windows, odd-angle siding, and unhinged doorways. The old house on the other side of the farm is falling down, but they don't care. Cutter doesn't come here and that makes it heaven.

I sense their dislike and distrust of me. I'm not like them. I never was and I never will be. They came to me in the beginning, trying to get me to go away with them—join them here—but I was afraid. They wear their naked, shredded skin like it's some kind of badge of unity.

I didn't want to see that. I didn't want to be reminded. I didn't want to be like them.

They are what they are by what he has done to them. He has changed them, created an endless circle of hate and fear for them to live in. I'm outside of that circle. I didn't look like them, not in the end. I am the only one who knows the horrors that come at the end—to not have any skin to wear at all. So, I look like me. And I'm not bound to the circle. I can leave and they can't. I can do what they can't. I am not one of them. At least, that's what I always thought.

Now, I hope that I'm wrong. I want to be seen as one of them because I need their strength.

I hope for a taste of vengeance, a taste for justice. And I hope they must as well.

I stop in front of the bowing, grey timbers of the porch and I wait. They seep out, slow and uncaring. Through moldy wall and decaying floorboard, drooping out of mouse-infested eaves. Like smoke and ants and slime. White bodies, gaping red wounds, dripping blood. So much blood.

Remembering all over why I'd run away from them when they'd come for me, I hold my breath and try not to tremble as their numbers grow.

So many.

In my more melancholy moments, I often wondered what it would be like if Cutter were actually recognized for his insane form of art. Our motley collection of gruesome art projects might be called "Cutter's Kids" and we'd go on a touring show in conjunction with the Bodies exhibit to New York City and London and Tokyo. People would stare at us with a strange mixture of morbid fascination and grotesque amusement.

I stare, watching as the last few art pieces come out for display. We're all sizes and genders, but always young. I don't think any of us are legally adults. Beyond wanting young flesh, Cutter didn't seem picky—as if he felt it was necessary to immortalize his work in all varieties of flesh. What does one whirling loop look like in the flesh of a five-month-old versus the flesh of an obese twelve-year-old or the muscles of an eighteen-year-old?

They stare at me with opaque white eyes. By all appearances, they look vengeful and terrifying. Yet, they don't haunt their killer or their place of death. We all died in The Room. I'm the only one brave enough to go back in there. I'm the only one brave enough to stay close to Cutter in the hopes of one day being able to dance on his unfortunate grave. I'm the one who held on, who bore it in silence, who lived. Until the very end.

They still stare, open-mouthed horrors who wear their last instant of agony.

"He's taken another," I finally say. My voice sounds strong to my own ears. Good, because I'm scared shitless. It's almost laughable for a ghost to be scared of ghosts, especially because they have no bone to pick with me. But they creep me out...especially the babies—naked and torn in the arms of a few of the older children. It makes my stomach crimp in on itself and I'm glad I can't throw up.

Their billowing white hair seems to seethe as heads turn and blank eyes search back and forth among one another. A matching army of confused zombies.

I continue. "I-I want to stop him."

Someone takes a step forward. A boy, close to my age. I can tell he was once just as tall and strong as I was, he probably thought he was an alpha just like I did. Cutter changed that for him. Just like he did for me. I can see it cut right out of his skin. Cutter treats men and women differently. I think he hates the males more; he relishes in emasculating us in his own special way—and that way hurts like hell.

The boy in front of me, incomplete as he is, cocks his head. He looks interested, like perhaps he's saying, "Go on." But then again, he also might be saying, "What the hell can you do?"

It's so hard to tell. None of them speak. I suspect they're broken-voiced.

Like Mia will soon be. I'm the only one that has a voice. I am the only one that didn't scream. I clenched my teeth against the pain until they broke and bled in my mouth, but I didn't scream. I wouldn't give Cutter that satisfaction. I glance over the bodies. None are as torn up as I was when I breathed my last breath. I lasted the longest. He told me as much, but here is my proof.

"I want you to help me," I say, rushing though the memories. "I need help to stop him."

As expected, I'm met with silence. For a moment, it's so still that all this seems like a heat mirage. The cicadas are deafening.

Finally, a girl with melancholy blank eyes—the same one who put her hand on my shoulder the other day—moves. A single left, right, left of her chin. No.

They start to seep back into their hidey-holes.

I hold out a hand and take a step toward them, "Wait!"

More sinking, faces puddling and becoming indiscernible before they glisten like spider web dew and disappear into nothingness. Evaporating in the heat. "Don't you want revenge?" I scream, running after them and trying to forcefully pull them back out into the open. "Don't you want to stop him?" I grasp at whispering hair. "Will you just let him keep killing more innocent people?" I dive for a hand.

I come up with nothing.

"If we don't do it then no one ever will and this will go on and on and our numbers will grow until the weight of us brings this house down!"

Nothing. Stillness. I'm still alone. The one line of defense against Cutter and his artistic madness.

# Twenty-Four:
# Corey

When I get back, Mia is still asleep. I don't think she's asleep at all. I think she has moved to a place of unconsciousness where Cutter's pain-making can't get her anymore.

I'm almost mad at him for being so sloppy with this job. He could have made her last longer if he took care of her. And then I would have more time to plan.

I have to act. I have to do whatever I'm going to do tonight. Because once he sees that he can't make pain for her, once he sees that her precious skin has gone paper thin, once he knows that she's no longer a viable body on which to ply his art, he'll kill her before the dehydration does.

I go out to the garden and pace back and forth between my neatly planted beds. What to do? What to do?

If I can't hurt him and the others will not help me, then I need to find someone who will.

But how? How am I going to recruit someone to help? Another ghost might...I could go trolling around the church graveyards or one of the older buildings in town. But who knows what kinds of rules bind other ghosts? I already know that I'm different than the ones here on the farm.

I might be the only ghost in town who can move from my place of death—able to garden, able to go sit in classrooms when I'm bored, or read books over the shoulders of library patrons, or sneak into movie theaters when new Marvel movies come out. I'm not caught in the circle. I'm still sort of alive, in my own way.

Could I get a human to help?

That would be best. However, it would be very dangerous to involve the living. Tangling anything alive up with Cutter probably isn't a good idea. And how would I get a human to follow me anyway?

\*\*\*

I'm still confused and puzzling over what to do when Cutter arrives home early. I run out of the garden and peg myself against him as he wearily takes his lunch cooler and some kind of bag I've never seen before from the truck.

He looks like ass. Not that Cutter was ever a looker to begin with. He's got bags under his eyes and he shuffles along like a man half asleep. Anxious, I follow him as he drags himself inside, sets everything down, and goes up to Mia.

Squatting beside her, he shakes her. When she doesn't stir, he begins taking her pulse and pulling up pinches of her skin. They stick up in slow-drooping peaks.

I hold my breath, expecting him to freak out again, but he doesn't.

Cutter takes out the key, unlocks Mia, and—astonishingly—picks her up and takes her to the bathroom. Using the same care as before, he strips her and lays her back in the bathtub. Then he turns on the spray and leaves her there.

I watch, mute and confused, as he changes the sheets and blankets. The mattress below is stained with feces, urine, and blood. A sick testament to his past transgressions. He covers them with fresh linens from the hallway closet. A pure, white mask over Death's fugly mug. He's not fooling anyone with that shit.

Cutter goes back into the bathroom and sets about cleaning Mia up. Except this time, I don't try to stop him because I'm confused. He never did this for me. And I doubt he did it for anyone. Is he trying to help her?

He doesn't whack off to her this time. Thank God. Even Cutter apparently has limits. I guess in his messed up little fantasy world, unconscious girls are okay, but half-dead ones are not. Seems weird that a sloppy murderer would have a taboo against necrophilia.

He cleans her up, dries her off, dresses her wounds—including smearing weird smelling stuff all over her bruised ribs and face, and slips her into a new ugly nightgown. Then, he carries her back to the bed and cuffs her back in.

He disappears from the room. I stay where I'm standing. Is he trying to cover up what he has done? Make it go away so he doesn't have to see? Is guilt at being a monster that easily covered up?

He comes back in, to my surprise, with an IV pole. A desperate scoff garbles up in my throat. "Are you fucking kidding me?"

I watch with wide-eyed amazement as Cutter expertly slips a needle into Mia's collapsed and dehydrated skin and hooks her up to an IV. He's giving her a chance. Rehydration.

Where did he even get that? Has it always been here? I don't know. I don't think I ever bothered checking the closets for that sort of thing. It hadn't occurred to me to check for hospital surplus, but now that I think about it, he always had bandages. He knows how to cut just right and keep someone alive...unless he's having a bad couple of days like he's been having with Mia. And Little Evie Lee—the favored sister—is a scalpel.

Is he some kind of modern day Jack the Ripper? Someone who actually knows medicine and instead of practicing it, turned it into something strange and deadly? A med school drop out turned tortured artist?

Is this Jekyll and Hyde?

Why do I care?

Cutter steps back, surveying his work, both good and bad, and leaves the room.

***

I stay with Mia for the whole night.

I'm both delighted and terrified that Cutter has done this for her. It means she'll live longer but it also mean's he'll torture her more.

She wakes up a little bit before dawn and blinks at me. "Corey?"

I wince at the sound of her voice, but try to hide it with a confident smile. "Hi."

Her gaze flies around the room.

"How are you feeling?"

Her eyes find mine again and trap them. I need to save this girl. "A little better."

"Good." Bad. Bad, bad, bad. "Go back to sleep." Go back under! Don't let him see you awake and alive! He'll only hurt you more. This is a sick game of cat and mouse—healing her only to hurt her. I hide all this morbid certainty under a smile for Mia.

Despite her split lips, she smiles back at me. I feel my heart melt down the inside of my ribcage and puddle at the bottom. Hollow boy with a heart of melted gold.

"Another...story? To sleep?" Her eyes are innocent and child-like in the grey light. I push her hair back behind her ear. I don't know where she's finding all this hope, all this faith. I never had any of that. But I do as she asks, because I understand her wanting to walk out of reality and find herself in someone else's life or fantasy.

I tell her about going abroad. Of trips that I went on with Mom and Dad. Dad was always away from home on business, but he did make good on taking off long stints so that we could have family time. Mom counted down the days on a calendar. Every two months, for one week, I had a father and she had her lover.

It was a time of magic and intrigue because my father never accepted the mundane or the boring. We went to cafés in Istanbul and the Louvre in Paris. We visited the ruins in Greece and I met some of my distant cousins in Naples. We climbed Arthur's Seat in Britain and dove in the reefs off of Hawaii. I held the sturdy body of a koala in Australia and swam with dolphins in the Keys. I learned how to waltz at a stuffy banquet in Moscow and went on safari in South Africa and visited an archaeological dig in Croatia.

Mia finally falls asleep, her head resting against my arm and her breath against my neck. I slide out from under her and kiss her forehead. And then I stand guard, waiting for the demon to awaken.

When Cutter comes in the morning, he barely even looks at Mia. He changes out the squeezed-flat Lactated Ringers Solution bag and exchanges it for a fat, lolling new one then goes to work.

Satisfied that Mia is safe for at least another few hours, I go to work.

# Twenty-Five:
# Corey

I walk out to the stop on the main road and catch a bus into town. I've done this at least a hundred times. It gets pretty boring living in Cutter's house, so I long ago figured I needed to get out and be with the people of the world. It makes me feel just a little bit normal. I sit between Joseph, the old man who always wears a fishing hat and goes to the library, and Marie, the hot housewife who sometimes cheats on her husband with a Shadwell United bank teller named Flo.

Yes, Flo is a woman.

I'm not telling. I'm not judging. On my better days, I find it incredibly hot, actually...and they don't seem to mind if I watch—which is cool of them.

Part of me knows it's perverted and wrong, but what horny eighteen-year-old wouldn't take advantage of being invisible and being able to walk through walls? Not this one.

Besides, they'll never, ever know and I'll never get in trouble for it.

Unless, of course, I eventually pass over and have my ass handed to me by the man upstairs.

But, because of how I died and the fact that I'm never going to be able to lose my virginity, I feel like I'm at least a little entitled to watch live-action hot lesbian sex every-so-often. And I feel like maybe whoever handles my case after I finally pass on will understand.

I get off at the Main Street stop and follow Joseph as far as the library. Normally, I'd go in with him and read over his shoulder. He likes mysteries and thrillers, I like standing near him when the hero is in a building filled with hostages and has to cut a bomb wire. He gets all sweaty and his heart starts beating—it reminds me of being alive. Not that my heart can't do these things, but up until Mia, life was pretty boring with Cutter.

Personally, I think it's because I do this that I still remember what it's like to be alive. I think it's why I still breathe and have a heart beat. I think that's why I'm warm and can still touch things and why Flo and Marie keep my plumbing in working order. I think that's maybe why I still look like normal...because I'm not consumed by death, but with life. And I never want to forget that. Because I want to be as alive as I can, even though I know I'm dead. I have so much more living to do. An eternity of it.

I watch Joseph push through the glass doors and continue on my way. At the police station, I slide past the bored looking woman in the kiosk and walk through the bolted doors. In the back, the desks are piled with files and surrounded by bulletin boards. I find the one I'm looking for.

It's Mia's missing person print out. The girl in the picture is nothing like the girl lying in the bed. I realize, for the first time, that Mia is beautiful.

She's bright and carefree, her smile easy, trusting, forgiving. If she ever gets out, she'll never smile like that again. So I feel like it's important to remember this girl in the picture for her. I owe her that much.

I stand there for a long moment, studying her face. When this picture was taken she never knew or thought that anything like what she has been through over the past few days could ever happen to her. People never think bad things could happen to them.

I didn't anyway.

According to this print out, Mia is like me. Swim team, National Honor Society, Class Council, Prom Committee. Smart, athletic, popular. This picture was taken with her in a nice dress—probably prom. The picture was cut out of a larger one, I can see the arm of whoever took her to the dance. I bet she has an alpha boyfriend not unlike how I used to be. It's probably that John guy she keeps crying out for when she sleeps.

I shake my head. Life was a game show and we were the lucky winners. Until Cutter literally cut us down to size. I glance at her home address. Jesus, she's far from home. But then again, so was I. Cutter's not stupid. He "goes the distance," as Cake would say.

I turn and study the few cops sitting in the room. One's flipping through pictures of a crime scene, another's typing at a computer, the last is sitting with his feet on his desk, playing with a slinky.

Nice to see our tax dollars at work.

I try the one at the computer. I push at his stapler, trying to get his attention. No go. This dude is engrossed. Good for you, Copper Man, at least someone is doing their job. I glance at what he's doing. Writing up some kind of report. Okay...

I crack my knuckles and lean through him, attempting for the first time to see if pushing means I can hit a button.

I think of being solid, something I always have to do if I want to do something like touch or sit. It feels really weird trying to be solid while leaning through someone's body. I punch at the *M* and am delighted to see a corresponding letter appear on the screen.

The man sitting inside of me deletes it almost instantly, as if he assumes he hit it accidentally. I try again, to no avail. Jeez, this guy is dense. I pound on the keys.

*jewhfowhjpfvoNWAIHOICFnwekf*

There. That should make him think he's not making typos. He draws in a breath and pulls his hands away. Seizing the opportunity, I type her name.

*Mia Lowell*

The cursor blinks after the keys fall silent, waiting.

He leans forward, stares at the keyboard, and rubs his eyes.

I type some more. *I know where she is. You have to save her.*

I have his attention now. He glances at his colleagues, trying to gauge if they are seeing what he's seeing. Frowning, he reaches out and slowly punches the keys one at a time, like an eighty-year-old who doesn't know how to use the computer, as if he expects the space bar to hop up and bite off his thumb. *Who are you?*

*It doesn't matter.* I punch in the address. *She's here. Kidnapped. Tied up. She needs help.*

He scowls. *I can't just go in there without any evidence. I need evidence for a search warrant.*

*There's no time. You'll find it when you get there. He's a killer. He killed a lot of people already.*

He seems confused and distressed at this. *Who is he? And who has he killed? How do you know?*

Wow, come to think of it, I don't even know Cutter's real name. Well, that's freaking not useful at all. *The Cutter.* Who? All of Cutter's Kids...but I don't know their names. All I know is Mia. And me... *He killed Corey Rossi.*

He seems very interested now. *How do you know? How can I trust you? Who are you?*

I hesitate for a moment. Aw, what the hell. *Because he killed me. I'm Corey Rossi.*

"Fuck," he growls, jumping to his feet.

I stumble back and wait, still as a cornered cat. I don't know what his reaction means. Does he believe me?

The cop with the crime scene pictures looks up. "Everything okay, Frank?"

Frank leans over and stabs at the delete button, erasing our conversation. "Yeah," he breathes. Now that I'm not practically sitting in his lap, I can see sweat beading on his forehead. "We've been hacked."

I slap my forehead. "Hacked? Really, Frank?"

The other officer sits forward. "What?"

Frank gestures at his computer. "Someone just hacked into my personal files and started jerking my chain around. Made the keys move on their own and everything."

Shit, well this was totally useless. I resist the urge to grab him by his dust-colored shirt and shake him. But what good would trying even do?

The cop with the slinky chuckles. "Sure, Frank. I think you need a vacation."

As the cops start ribbing each other, I shove out of the station and take to the streets. What now? Try something else? I walk across lawns and through houses, uncertain of what I could do.

Should I try going to her parents? They'd probably believe me if I tried. But that far away? And what's to keep the cops from brushing them off and insisting that they're coming up with solutions where they don't exist?

I breeze through someone's kitchen. It's a house with young children. I can tell that instantly. There are those primary-colored alphabet magnets on the fridge. I stop short, an idea in my head. I begin shoving letters around on the fridge, making do with the letters I've got and no numbers.

## HELP MIA
## AT FARM

Grinning, I move on. Building momentum as I go house to house and block to block. Spelling out my message in any medium I can get. Knocking over flour and writing on the floor, using pens and pencils and straws to spell out rickety words on counters. I hit at least three dozen houses before I realize what time it is and have to go home before Cutter gets back.

I don't know if it's enough.

I can only hope.

# Twenty-Six:
# Sydney

John suddenly gets up, startling everyone at the table. "Fuck this," he growls. "Fuck this shit. I can't sit here any more."

I glance at my parents. Neither seem to have heard his outburst, though that doesn't surprise me.

Mom is completely void of any life; her normally perfect hair has gone unwashed for days, she's wearing wrinkled, stinky pajamas, and only seems to move when she clutches at the nearest person's hand.

Dad's not much better. His gaze keeps flicking from the front window to the phone, then back to Mom, and finally to me—his expression wild and confused, as if he's uncertain who he should be more concerned about and is looking to me to solve it.

Nick is the one who looks up from his untouched turkey sandwich and speaks. "What are you talking about?"

Lifting his hand to his head and grabbing a fist full of hair, John glares at the table and says, "I can't just sit here waiting for news any more. I need to do something."

Nick gestures at the stacks of fliers sitting between us like piss-poor centerpieces. "We've *been* doing something."

In response, John lurches forward and swats the fliers off the table. They flap all over the dining room, landing around us like an uneven dusting of snow. "This is useless. We're not even putting them up in the right area!"

I bite my lips and pick at the fraying edge of my place mat. He's right, of course. The proper place to put these would be near where Mia went missing, but I can't get there. I don't even have my permit yet. I rub my arm, feeling useless.

John straightens, looking at each one of us in turn. His gaze seems to linger on my parents, huddled together at the end of the table, the haunted refugees of their own personal nightmare. "You can all sit here and wait for bad fucking news, but I'm going to look for her."

With that, he turns on his heel and heads out of the dining room.

Without thinking, I clamber to my feet and jog after him. "Wait! John, wait!"

He pauses on the sidewalk, his back tense as if fighting against invisible rope, his fists balled. I'm holding him against his task. "What?" he barks.

I feel myself cower slightly, made useless and afraid by this whole ordeal. I curl my toes against my flip flops; I can feel the hot pavement through the thin plastic. "I-I'm coming with you."

He's quiet for a long moment before turning and giving me a calculating sidelong glance. I meet his eyes, trying to look confident and insistent. His expression seems to say, "No way in hell," so I plead my case.

"I have just as much of a right to look for her as you do." His chin tenses and I don't know whether that's a good thing or bad, so I say, "And...you're right. I'm sick of waiting for something to happen."

I hear Nick speak from the doorway. "Just let her go, man."

John turns away, his hand clenching around his keys. "Fine. We're leaving straight away. Go pack what you need, I'll be back to pick you up in an hour."

# Twenty-Seven:
# Corey

Cutter has come home, changed Mia's fluids and is eating dinner when a knock comes at the door. I hover close to Cutter as he answers the door. I'm surprised to see Officer Frank on the other side. Thank you, Jesus!

But then I realize he's dressed in civilian clothes and parked just beyond the porch is an unmarked car. Where's the SWAT team?

"Wayne Howley?"

Cutter grunts. "Yeah, that's me."

Frank puts his hand in his pocket and pulls out his badge. "Officer Frank Stapleton. You mind if I come in?"

Cutter seems to deliberate this for a long moment. He shoves the door wider. "Sure."

Frank steps into the kitchen and takes a quick glance around. "Nice place you got here. Nice...and remote."

Cutter goes back to the table and sits again. "I like quiet. Don't like to be bothered."

Frank flashes a quick, depreciative smile.

Cutter gives him a narrow eye, takes a bite and then talks around it, "You mind telling me why you're here?"

Frank shrugs, his eyes lingering around the room as if cataloguing all the possible tells that make Cutter a sociopathic murderer. "You wouldn't believe it actually. I got the strangest message today. It's just an unofficial little checkup."

Huh. So either my little "prank" finally got to dear old Frank's conscience or he'd gotten word of what I'd done in the houses. Maybe I even hit his house and freaked him and the missus out when they got home. Even so, how unofficial is this? Does anybody even know Frank's out here doing this? Did he just decide to look into it himself?

Cutter shovels the final spoonful of instant mashed potatoes into his mouth and stands to put his plate in the sink. "So, what are we checking on?"

Frank steps a little closer, as if trying to intimidate Cutter. It's a stupid idea. "You ever hear of a girl named Mia Lowell?"

Cutter's face remains completely stoic. "Nope."

I expect that. I doubt he knows the name of the girl upstairs.

"How about a Corey Rossi?"

Won't know me either.

Cutter glances over his shoulder, his face a mask that I don't understand. I've never seen that expression on his face before. "No. Why? What'd they do? Up and run away together?"

I wish. I don't even know if Mia will be able to use her leg again.

Frank stares at him for a long moment. "They're missing persons. Don't you watch the news, Mr. Howley?"

Cutter gestures toward the living room. "I ain't got a television. Rots your brain."

"So," Frank says, shoving his hands in his pocket and doing a slow walk across the kitchen, "what do you do out here all alone?"

Cutter turns and smiles at him. All snake-oil. "I'm an artist. And I collect knives, go hunting and fishing. You wanna see my trophies and my favorite pieces?"

Frank seems ignited by this idea, probably a chance to explore more of the house and look for clues. What a hack. *Go back to the mystery mobile, Scooby.* "Sure."

Cutter gestures for Frank to follow him into the living room. Cutter has knives, stuffed fish, and glassy-eyed heads mounted on the wall here. He does hunt and he does fish and he most certainly collects knives. But these are not his babies, not his prized trophies, not his artisan blades. He explains each blade to intricate boredom, tells the tale of each buck and each big mouth bass. I'm half asleep when he leads Frank into the back room.

Cutter was, long ago, a for-real artist. He was a sculptor, taking discerning slices out of formless clay. He was a painter, brushing oil and acrylic along delicately rendered human forms. I know the pieces in the backroom are his because I recognize his style in the whorls and zags. But, for whatever reason, at some point a long time ago, Cutter put down his canvas and took up skin, put down his loop and took up a blade. Perhaps he thought the soul had gone out of his work and he figured he could substitute that soul by literally bringing life into his art.

In some ways he succeeded.

I mean, aren't all of us Kids his pieces? Souls wearing his mark? The abandoned house on the other side of the farm is his grizzly art gallery.

Frank seems surprised by the studio. "I definitely would not have pegged you as an artist, Mr. Howley, but you're pretty good."

Cutter smiles. "I'm just full of surprises. Let me show you this one over here." He reaches out and, taking Frank by the shoulder, guides him further into the room. As they pass a table thickly layered with dried shavings and glops of clay, Cutter's free hand slides over the grey-brown dust and finds an old abandoned tool. It's covered in flakey clay fingerprints and it's a little rusty, but I'm not blind. After careful tutelage under Cutter and The Sisters, I know blades like I know breath.

On instinct, I leap forward, trying to grab Cutter's hand, but it's too late. He's so fast. Too fast. The sculpting tool comes up and over and just like that, blood is spurting in arcs over the scattered canvases—forever tainting Cutter's past art style with his new one.

As Cutter lets Frank fall to the floor, he lifts his new weapon and grins at it. "My favorite piece," Cutter giggles. "I call it Rhapsody in Red."

\*\*\*

After that, as he's cleaning up Frank's body, Cutter won't stop alternately giggling and whistling "Rhapsody in Blue."

Seething with hate, I sit slumped in the corner and glare at him. I had not wanted it to go this way. I had wanted to get Mia out, not get another person killed. But, to be fair, this is a new MO for Cutter. I've never thought of him as someone prone to spontaneous murder, it doesn't go with his artistic psychosis. But then, I guess everyone changes.

I lower my head and rub my palms into my eyes. "It's all my fault."

Someone grasps my shoulder. Startled, I pull away and glance up. Officer Frank is standing beside me, one hand on his hip and frowning down at Cutter. "It's my fault, kid. I should have listened to you."

I don't respond. I don't know what to say to that. We just watch as Cutter hacks up Frank's body and tosses the bits into an empty trash can.

"What's he going to do with me?" Frank asks, wincing a bit as Cutter takes a hammer to his skull.

I shrug. "I don't know. I never saw where he took me." I trail my eyes back down to the shrinking pile of charnel that used to be a human body. Will he take Frank to the same place he took me or does he dump everyone someplace different?

Cutter drops the last of Frank's remains into the garbage bin and plops the lid in place. There's a streaky, slightly chunky puddle on the floor and blood all over the walls and Cutter's art. He doesn't seem to care about cleaning it up.

Instead, he collects the carving tools and heads into the kitchen. Frank and I trail behind him. He dumps the whole handful into the sink and washes each one until not a speck of clay remains. Completely ignoring his dinner dishes and the car still parked in his driveway, Cutter turns—new instruments in hand—and heads up to The Room.

I go upstairs, too, but I don't go in. I can't. I can't see her getting hurt again, it might kill me all over.

Frank hovers close, as if he's not sure how to do this ghosting business. He's like me. Not marred by the wounds of his death, not confused as to what happened to him.

I can hear Cutter's voice from within, though I can't hear what he says. Mia begins moaning in pain. I press myself against the wall and squeeze my eyes shut. I wish I could evaporate into nothing. I wish I had no ears. I wish I had no heart—because then it wouldn't be breaking.

"What's going on? Aren't you going to do something?" Frank demands.

I flash him a silent snarl. Doesn't he get it?

He slips away from my side, shoving into The Room. Intent on being a hero, no doubt. Let him realize there is nothing that he can do.

Though, with all my trembling fibers of non-being, I hope that he can do what I can't.

He emerges a few minutes later, eyes wide and haunted, shaking and pale. He slumps against the wall and sinks to the floor. I go with him. The will to stand has left me.

# Twenty-Eight:
# Corey

Later, once Cutter has released his muse and silence envelops the house, I stand. It's too quiet and Cutter should have come out by now. I lean against the wall and slide into The Room. A moment later, Officer Frank appears beside me.

Cutter is hunched over Mia, wrapping her other leg. She's unconscious again, driven to blank emptiness by shock.

"What the hell is going on?" Frank asks.

I don't answer him for a long moment. To be honest, I really don't know. Perhaps, now that Cutter tasted what it's like to finally finish a piece, he's learned that he needs to care more for them. I know I was that piece. Not only because I remember Cutter telling me so, but because I lived the longest out of all of Cutter's Kids. I'm the only one that lived for two weeks and I'm the one with the most cuts. I lived because I guess that I thought that maybe I'd be saved or he'd let me go once he was done. But it didn't happen like that.

What do you do when you finish a piece of art? You hang it on the wall.

And that's how I died. Unlike the others who died of dehydration and infection and blood loss and shock and being cut up, I died while I was being skinned alive.

A shiver runs up my spine and makes my flesh break out in goosebumps. Cutter got his glory with me, he tasted victory and finally got his trophy. He wants it again—with Mia. He's keeping her alive so he can finish the job...so she can die like I did. In something worse than this.

"We have to help her," I say.

Frank blinks at me like I'm an idiot. "Well yeah, obviously."

Cutter suddenly straightens. He sighs, cracks his neck and stretches his arms over his head. He's covered in blood, both Mia's and Franks, and he's got an insane grin on his face. He collects up his tools and heads out of the room. We follow him.

"So, what do you propose we do?" Frank asks.

I scowl to myself. I don't know. "Did anyone know you were coming here?"

Frank makes a strangled expression, which I take to mean no.

I look away, annoyed with him. "So you just thought you'd come in here, push him until he cracked and then take him down, gun blazing with vigilante justice? Well, I donno if you've noticed, but we're dealing with the next H.H. Holmes here." I gesture at Cutter who is dragging the trash bin across the living room. The heavy barrel scrapes across the floor, dragging up slivers of wood.

Frank doesn't humor me with an answer.

We watch in frustrated silence as Cutter drags the barrel to the basement door, opens the door and topples the whole thing into the dark pit of the basement. It lands on the cement floor with a reverberating metallic clang. A second later, I hear Delilah digging in.

"Son of a bitch," I breathe.

Frank steps closer. "What?"

"He fed me to a fucking mastiff." No wonder I could never find any bodies. That dog is starved for such long intervals that she chews bones down to nothing. Come to think of it, when I first started haunting this house and discovered the poor monster in the basement, I shoved the meaty bones closer to her. Jesus...I gave her my own body parts to chew on.

Cutter shuts the basement door, closing off the sound of Delilah chomping on Frank's remains, and returns to cleaning. But neither Frank nor I move. We just stand, staring at the basement door.

# Twenty-Nine: Corey

It's weird having a partner in crime. Especially when he's three times your age and a cop. It kind of makes you nervous even though you're pretty sure his ghost-cuffs won't stay on you and his ghost gun won't kill you...you're already dead, after all.

Mia has been unconscious for hours. Frank and I sit in The Room and watch her, two miserable sentinels.

"We have to do something," Frank says. His voice sounds weak. I'm sure he's not used to feeling this useless.

"What do you want to do," I say, feeling bitter and snarky, "call the cops?"

Frank purses his lips and rubs his chin. "It's not a bad idea, could do what you did with me."

I roll my eyes. "You didn't believe me, remember? And your cop buddies thought you were nuts."

Frank's quiet for a long moment. "It was the other stuff you did. I started getting reports of break-ins that weren't break-ins. Minimal damage, random notes about Mia and a farm."

I nod to myself. "Nice to see something was useful."

"We could try it again," Frank ventures.

"And risk some other idiot cop coming sniffing around Cutter's door? You really hate your friends that much? I'm not risking anyone else's life."

Frank sighs. "Then what?"

I get up and go to Mia's side. Cutter didn't give her fluids after he went to bed. I think he wants to keep her riding the line between dead and alive. I reach out and smooth her hair, which even in the small time she has been here has turned from smooth, lustrous golden silk to an oily, dry mass of old straw. I try to find the beauty from her photo under the lines of pain, but she seems irreparably uglied by this ordeal. "How long do you think she'll live?"

"What?" Frank barks. "Why do you want to know that?"

I glance over my shoulder. "I want to know if she'll be alive when I get back."

# Thirty:
# Corey

I have a plan. It's my last, desperate hope, but I don't know what else to do. I take the local bus to another stop, hop the next bus to the rest stop and wait there for another promising mode of transport.

I slide through the glass doors and weave among the people standing at kiosks and taking up space on the tan tiles. Some are holding Dunkin' Donuts cups, others are practically running to the rest room, and a couple look ragged and drooping—half ready to nose dive into their Subway sandwiches and trays of dollar menu fries.

When I get close to the map with the little "You Are Here" sticker on it, I stare up at it, trying to figure out the best route to take while eavesdropping on the people around me—watching eyes and fingers trace interstates and back roads, hoping to find someone going in my direction.

I doubt there's anyone that will get me exactly to Mia's hometown, so I'm going to need to hop cars. And I need to make sure I plan it all out correctly otherwise I'll end up in Wyoming or something. I'm complaining to myself about how I wish I could just ask someone where they're going when a ribbon of conversation catches my attention.

"Mia's car was found about ten miles east of here."

I spin around. There's a short, chubby girl with blond dreads briskly walking toward the exit. A tall, wiry guy is trailing after her, his eyes on a smart phone. "Right, I got it pinned on my Google maps."

The girl doesn't answer, so he lowers the phone and calls after her, "Sydney, hold up a second."

The girl—Sydney—pauses, her hand white knuckled on her purse. "What? We're losing time." For a split second, they glare at each other, the air around them crackling with intensity. I'm not the only one whose attention their volatile energy has attracted.

The wiry guy glances around and takes a deep breath, visibly trying to lower his tense, broad shoulders. "If we make a plan of action, we'll find her faster."

Sydney closes her eyes and lowers her chin, her hand slides off of her hippie bag and she takes a step to face him. "You're right."

He tucks his phone into his back pocket, a short quick gesture that seems more like a punctuation mark than anything I've ever seen. "I know."

She smirks, her blue eyes weary but somehow laughing. "You two are infuriatingly alike."

A slight smirk tugs at his lips, flashing a dimple. "I know that, too."

Abandoning the map, I step closer to the girl, scrutinizing her. At first glance, I wouldn't associate her with Mia, but...close up, I can see similarities between the two. Same bone structure, same eyes. Wanting to be certain, I check the initials on her bag. S.L. Maybe the L means Lowell? Maybe she's Mia's sister, or a cousin?

I glance at the boy. No familial resemblance, but there's something about him that makes me feel he's closer to Mia than most. Something in his rigid stance and the expression on his face. Desperation and longing. And that class ring...this must be the owner of the arm that Mia's smiling about in that missing person's picture. I'd bet my life on it...well, my non-life, I guess. Maybe it's this John guy.

"So," Sydney says, "what did you have in mind?"

He nods to himself, as if getting back on track. "I think we should go to where she was lost, do an examination of the surrounding area."

Sydney frowns. "Don't you think that if there was something there, the police would have picked it up?"

He shrugs, his eyes sliding off to the side to examine the little paper pamphlets advertising the attractions in this area. "You have a better idea?"

Sydney unconsciously plays with a tongue ring for a moment, the silver ball flashing between her lips. "No. Not really."

"Okay then." He brushes past her and heads toward the door. "We'll get there, look around. If we don't find anything then let's look at the closest towns."

Sydney nods at his back as she trails him. On a whim, I follow him, too, and when he gets to a red Mazda, I don't hesitate to get into the back seat.

He puts his phone into a little holder on the dash board and I'm pleased to see that my suspicions about who he is are true when his background image settles on Mia's smiling face.

I wait as he taps up his GPS app and it orients itself. The automated voice prompts him and he gets on the highway.

Sydney and the boy are quiet for a long time. Sydney rolls her dreads between her fingers, he bounces his free leg and taps at his knee.

Eventually, Sydney says, "Hey, John?" Ah, I thought right! This is John!

"Yeah?"

"What do you think we'll find?"

John shrugs. I'm sure he's hoping nothing. At least nothing like a dead body in a ditch. It never occurred to me that of the people in her life that would come looking for Mia, her little sister and her boyfriend would be the ones. But, I suppose it makes sense. Where are her parents?

John's phone rings then, the screen lighting up. Frowning, he tips it toward Sydney who rolls her eyes and makes a disgusted noise at what she reads. John pulls it off of the dash and picks it up anyway. "Hi, Ti."

A high-pitched string of babbling occurs on the other side of the line as John half-heartedly checks his mirrors and pulls off into the median.

After a long moment, silence falls and John sighs. "Yes, I thought about asking if you wanted to come." Babble, babble, babble. "No. Look, you're the last person Syd wants around right now." More high-pitched chittering. "Well, I wonder why she thinks it's your fault, Ti? Is it?" Silence on the other side, then a low-pitched syllable.

John, cradling the phone with his shoulder, rubs his forehead with one hand. Ti says something else, her voice a little calmer and broken. "Ti, don't cry. We'll find her."

A wailing sort of babble responds. I think I hear, "It's all my fault!" but it's hard to tell.

John's fingers tap the steering wheel, which looks to me like he's mentally counting—looking for patience. When he speaks, his voice is tight. "Look, I know you feel like it's your fault. We all feel a little to blame. I could have stopped her; I saw her leaving. And Syd feels like she should have convinced her to come home that night and her parents are mad they let her go to your party in the first place. But the bottom line is that it happened. We just have to find her. I'm going to find her." He says this with such certainty that I suddenly know what has to happen.

I have to get this boy to follow me. Because I honestly believe he'll do it. He's going to save Mia Lowell. He'd kill to get her back, and that's exactly what he needs to do.

John talks to Ti for a few minutes more then hangs up.

As he pulls back onto the highway, Sydney says, "What did that skank want?"

John gives her a quick sidelong glance as he accelerates. "She wanted to know why we didn't ask her to come with us."

Sydney scoffs and crosses her arms. "God, she's dumb."

"She just wants to help, Syd. You can't keep slamming the door in her face and ignoring her calls. She has a right to want to find Mia, too. They're best friends. One fight can't possibly change that."

Sydney's eyes scrunch into an ugly expression and I can tell that Sydney has true feelings of hate toward this Ti girl. "Ti gave up her rights to friendship when she did what she did to Mia."

John examines her for an instant, brown-green eyes calculating, before he has to look back at the road. "You're serious, aren't you?"

"Did you think I wasn't?"

John looks mildly guilty for an instant. "I may have thought you might be blowing things out of proportion."

Sydney clenches her jaw. "It's been a long time since I did anything like that."

He sighs. "Yeah, I know." Then, after a moment, he says, "You wanna tell me exactly what happened with those two?"

Sydney turns her head and stares at him for a long, long moment. I try to understand her expression, but I don't think I've ever seen a face embodying that pinched mouth and those wide eyes before. "No, John, I don't. And honestly, you really don't want to know."

He frowns, a challenge in his brows, before he shakes his head. "You're right. It's none of my business."

Defeated—probably by his utter selflessness toward Mia—Sydney closes her eyes and lowers her head, her hair sliding like a beaded curtain between them. "No. It is your business. You're doing all of this for Mia...and you should know. They had a fight about William Carrig."

I sense John's body go tense, his jaw muscles becoming more pronounced under his taut cheek. He balls his fist against his leg, making the veins in his arms stand out. "Is that who she left me for?"

Sydney doesn't answer, but her silence is an obvious yes. Then she whispers, "I'm sorry, John."

He shrugs, his eyes avoiding hers at all costs. "It doesn't matter." But it does matter. To this John guy, it matters very much. You'd be deaf, dumb, and blind not to see it.

I know it's kind of gay to want to give another guy a hug, but right now? I wish I could hug John. Because what he's thinking? That Mia has abandoned their love is the farthest thing from the truth.

I wish I could somehow tell him that Mia loves him still, that above all these other people in Mia's life, it's him who she calls out for in her sleep.

# Thirty-One:
# Sydney

John's Mazda sits ticking a couple of hundred yards away as he and I trudge down a cracked grey road with rows of corn on either side and not a building to be seen. I glance around. No wonder Mia couldn't tell me exactly where she was.

"Where'd they put her car?" John asks.

I frown, trying to remember what the police had said. "They towed it. It's impounded somewhere—for evidence, I think. Mom and Dad will have it shipped home once we...once we..."

"We'll find her," John says almost absently as his eyes scan the ground. He walks a few paces and points at something. "This must be it."

I follow his gesture to where the grass and mud on the side of the road have more footprints and tire tracks than anywhere else. I can see deep paw prints leading into the corn, they must have gone through with tracking or cadaver dogs or something.

I take a step toward the tracks, responding to a sudden instinct to follow them.

I stop short.

I don't want to see...not really. What if there's blood? What if...what if... Oh, I don't know! My heart is beating so fast, my breath all of a sudden is too hard to catch. A thick drop of sweat trails down my neck.

John stops a moment after me and glances over his shoulder. His eyes seem to ask if I'm okay and then he sees that I can't do this. He nods and turns around, going forward without me. Being braver than I am. I should be able to do this, shouldn't I? I came here to be helpful—to verify that this is indeed real. But now that I'm here, I don't want it to be real. I want this all to be a very bad dream. One that I'm going to wake up from at any moment.

As John stands in the middle of the chaos, his eyes tracking the comings and goings of invisible persons past, I squeeze my eyes shut and wish to God.

*Please, please, please let Mia be okay. Let us find her. Help us find her.*

Something taps my shoe. I ignore it, choosing instead to knit my fingers together and pray harder. I never really put much faith in God and prayer. But that doesn't matter when you're at the end of your rope and dangling over the precipice of something terrible. It doesn't matter when you're desperate. You pray, and you hope, and you wish for there to indeed be something bigger out there. Something that will listen and take mercy on your situation. You'd dedicate yourself to a force that powerful. You'd do anything. I understand now why people sell their souls.

*Help me. Not even me. Help my sister. Please.*

Something else taps my shoe. And then another.

Certain now that a bug or something is highly confused or that a mouse might crawl up my leg, I pop my eyes open and look down. At my foot are three large stones and just beside them, tiny sticks shaped like an arrow.

170

An arrow pointing in a particular direction.

I cock my head, uncertain if I'm seeing things, and stare at the debris by my foot.

"Syd," John calls.

I don't look up. Is this a sign? Something from God?

"You okay?" John asks. I hear him crunching over and before I can really think about it, I scrub my foot through the arrow. "What are you looking at?"

I force my eyes up. "Nothing." I don't want to admit to what I saw. That would mean I'm having delusions again, right? He examines me hard. I always was a bad liar. So, I try to derail him, "Did you find anything?"

He shakes his head, a swath of hair tumbling over his eyes. "Nothing that I'm certain the police haven't already found."

I bite my tongue ring. "What now?"

"Well, to the nearest town I guess." He turns in the direction he came from. "I think maybe the one we passed through a few miles back is the closest."

I glance in the other direction. The one that the arrow pointed in. Should I trust it? What if I'm just seeing things because I want to see them? But I've been taking my meds and I've been fine for a while now. I shouldn't be having hallucinations. But, if I'm to honestly believe that what I just saw was true, that would mean I believe that God is aiding my cause...and my therapist would say that's me convincing myself of a non-truth.

As if hearing my thoughts, Maybe-God taps my foot again. The sticks are back in their arrow, this time tighter and more certain.

I look up at John and meet his eyes—which seem sort of concerned. Does it matter if I'm insane? Maybe, just maybe, this is a sign? Something good? Maybe these arrows are telling me the truth. I ball my fists, terrified that I'm actually going to pay attention to them. But I'm just that desperate. "I think we should go this way."

John frowns at me. "That's not part of the plan."

"I know," I say with a shrug as I subtly toe the sticks out of order, "but I just have a feeling."

John stares a me for a long time. He's that quiet thinker type, always calculating, always thinking before opening his mouth. "A gut feeling?"

I shove my hand in my pockets, uncomfortable with admitting that I just might be following signs from God...or my insanity... Inside my pocket, my fingers find the old fortune. I really should learn to wash my clothes; I'm going to start to smell.

Wait...I pull the fortune out, read it over once more and glance at the sticks next to my converses. Somehow, they're back in an arrow *again*, pointing in the same direction. I want to believe. That's what Nick said, isn't it? I nod. "I really think we should go that way, John. I *know* it."

As if that's all John needed to hear, he says, "Okay," and heads back toward his Mazda. "Come on, we're losing daylight."

# Thirty-Two:
# Mia

They stand over me, watching and waiting. I know who each and every one of them are. Not their names, not where they are from, or what their lives were like. I know them by their true identities, the thing that made them who they were in the end. The thing that they will be remembered for.

The tortured.

The dead ones.

The victims of the blade.

I recognize the marks on them. Whorls, lines, etches...things that bleed, things that swell, things that infest you with heat and bee stings. Demonic art that breathes and bleeds.

I mentally name each piece...

The Wounded stands to my left.

The Lacerated just beside him, like a little girlfriend.

The Cut holds The Stabbed's hand. I can't look into The Stabbed's eyes, she's too little.

The Butchered stands at the end of the bed, tall and screaming like a banshee...an angel of death...a harbinger of impending doom.

The Hacked looms in the corner of the room like a punished kid, as if uncertain why he's here.

They've all come, cycling in and out as if I'm the one on exhibition...the centerpiece of the gallery. I wonder what they call me. The Frightened? The Captive? The Tortured? The Dying?

But what's in a name?

Nothing you could call me explains what's inside of me.

And even though these are empty shells, no words fully explain what they are—who they have become—either.

No word or thought or empathetic feeling could embody the thousand little things that made them different from the rest of the world.

All I know is that I don't want to be like them. I don't want a tragic, embodying name like The Slain. I don't want to be one of them.

The other victims. The other kids that Cutter killed. I know them. Whether they are a truth or an imagined nightmare is irrelevant. They aren't here to help—I know this for a certainty. It's like they've come to verify their own existence. To be certain that their own end wasn't a dream.

They aren't comforting—not like Corey. They aren't benevolent, not like the new stranger who sits on the edge of the bed, face stony and determined as a gargoyle. He watches them, mouth grim...face...frightened. Even imaginary ghosts are afraid of these creatures.

They are haunts. Taunts. Demons. Showing me what I will be. In hours, in days. Whenever I give up living. I will join their ranks.

It's their presence above anything else that keeps me alive.

I see the frozen expressions of agony, wide eyes full of blood, gaping mouths screaming dark emptiness, taloned fingers clawing at the air, and I force myself to keep breathing.

My eyes trace the lines in their skin, sisters to the ones I wear. Beatific, horrific scarifications that never healed, that glisten fresh with blood and pus. Bare skin and festering wound. And I focus on the blood pounding in my ears, making my head ache, and I welcome the pain because it means I'm still there.

I count them. One, two, three, four...and each time I wait for my heartbeat to match them. Once around the room, back the other way. Thump, thumping out a ballad of, "I am not dead. I won't be dead. You can't make me. I refuse."

When Cutter's feet take the stairs, I say "Live. Live. Live." Twenty-one times. That's how many steps.

When Cutter whistles his song, I sing my own song...

*I won't die, your sisters can't take the life from me;*
*I won't die, your scissors and blades can't take the soul*
*from me;*
*And although you try, your efforts won't strip my*
*breath away...*

I say, "No." Out loud, in my head, with every stroke of the knife when Cutter comes into my torture chamber.

The taunts stand around him, watching with the detached interest of the dead. No emotion save the horror-struck expressions that fleeting breath left them with. They huddle close, like hungry monsters starved and expecting a meal. Beckoning me to join them. And I tell them, "No."

His sisters cut into me, taste me, bathe in my blood like the vile teeth of Lady Bathory, and I tell them, "No."

He grins, leering bright teeth, his hands harsh, his breath stinking and labored as if this were an arousal and I say to him, "No."

Darkness folds in around my eyes, The Reaper stands ready in the corner with his scythe, the bright light explodes from the center beckoning me to the great beyond, and I tell them both, "No."

I will not die. I can not die. I refuse to die. I will not join these ghosts of frozen torture. I will not let The Sisters drain me dry. I will not give Cutter my soul. I will not let The Reaper have me. I won't succumb to the darkness. I will not walk into the white light.

Keep breathing lungs.

Keep resisting.

Keep pumping heart.

Keep living.

Keep flowing blood.

Keep running away, away, away...away.

Someone help me. Please help me.

# Thirty-Three:
# Sydney

I trudge behind John as we alternate stapling up missing person fliers and going door to door showing people pictures of my sister and asking if anyone has seen her.

"Are you all right?" John asks.

I blink at him, blurry eyed. I'm exhausted. This is the third town we've been to today. Thank goodness that all the towns around here consist mainly of a broken down little main street with half a dozen small shops. "Yeah, I'm just tired."

He frowns at me, deepening the worry lines that seem to have aged him by a decade in just a few days. "Maybe you should sit down and take a breather. I'll do the rest of the street and then we'll stop for the night."

I can tell John doesn't want to stop at all; he'd go forever if he could, but it's almost dark and most of the stores are closed right now. Grateful for his mercy, I stop and lean against the brick wall of the nearest building. I haven't gotten much sleep since Mia disappeared. How could I? How can I ever rest again?

I watch John go into a kitschy little gift shop with psychotic-faced figurines in the window before taking out my phone and calling Nick.

"Hey," he says after two rings. "I was wondering when you were going to call me."

I try not to feel guilty.

"How's the search going?"

I shrug. "Okay, I guess."

"Any leads."

I wipe the sweat off my brow. "No."

He's quiet for a moment. "Well, you can't expect any right away."

"It's been two days."

More quiet. "Well, at least you're out there doing something, right?"

"Yeah," I agree.

"So," he continues, his voice sounding like he's not entirely sure how to talk about this. "What kind of plan are you guys following?"

I poke at the bricks in the wall, stalling for a moment while I try to figure out how to explain how we got to this particular town. Aw hell... "Would you believe me if I told you I'm following God?"

Nick is quiet for a long moment. Then he says, "Quit joking."

My heart sinks. "I'm serious, Nick. I'm sort of...seeing signs."

"Signs?"

"Yes. Like signs from God?" Or, what I'm more afraid of, signs from Mia's ghost. Or, what I'm even more afraid of...signs of my own insanity.

More silence. A bad silence, one in which I know I should have just told Nick a lie. "Syd, are you joking with me?"

Sighing, I rub one of my eyes. "I really wish I was joking, Nick. But I'm seriously seeing things. Arrows, notes...this morning Mia's name was written on the bathroom mirror with a big arrow pointing in this direction."

More silence. "Have you told John?"

"No," I bark. "He'll want to turn around and take me home."

"You *should* come home," Nick snaps back. Then he chooses his words very carefully. "Look, you're obviously under a lot of emotional stress."

I roll my eyes. "Stop being my shrink, Nick. I know I sound nuts, but I'm taking my meds and nothing else is being weird. I'm just seeing signs and I really believe they'll lead me to Mia. I'll worry about possibly having an acute episode *after* we find my sister. Now, how are my parents?"

"Don't change the subject," he admonishes.

"We're not talking about this anymore. How. Are. My. Parents?" I emphasize, brooking no argument.

He growls to himself on the other side. "They're okay I guess. I think your dad managed to get your mom to eat something this morning. I'd really prefer not to spy on your parents, you know?"

I get up and wander toward the outdoor displays that one of the shops put out to draw in customers. "But you're doing it because you're the best person in the whole world." I finger a row of old books set out on a wheeled shelf. I get the general idea from the junk that this is a thrift or consignment shop.

He huffs. "You owe me."

I smirk. "I can think of a couple of ways to pay you back," I tease.

179

Suddenly, something comes flying off of the top shelf of a cart, making me jump and gasp.

"Syd?" Nick asks. "You okay?"

I stare down at what just kamikaze dive bombed me. It's a game. "Nothing, I just knocked something off of a shelf." I shake my head, denying my lie. I didn't touch that game; it literally came flying at me.

Unnerved, I bend down and reach for the bottom of the box and the folded board inside falls open. It's a Ouija board.

"So, where are you right now?"

I reach for the plastic magnifier. "Some Podunk town in the middle of—" I pause, voice caught. Because the magnifier just slid away from me. I reach for it again, but it slides out of my fingers and jumps up on the board.

"Middle of?" Nick prompts, but I don't answer him. "Syd?" But I hardly hear him, the phone is sinking away from my ear as I watch the magnifier slide across the board.

*M-I-A.* I blink at it. It repeats itself. Over and over. Nick is yelling my name now, voice frantic.

I snap myself out of it and lift the phone. "I have to go. I'll call you back." I practically slam the phone down on the ground as I drop to my knees. Staring.

It's still going. *Mia. Mia. Mia.*

I glance around, wondering if anyone else is seeing this, but I'm between two tall carts of junk, and this town is practically dead on a weekday evening. Everyone is probably home having dinner.

My phone vibrates, Nick calling me back no doubt. I ignore him.

Feeling like an idiot, I bend closer to the board. "Yes?!" I hiss. "What about her? Where is she?" I can't believe I'm talking to a game board.

The piece goes still for an instant, hovering between I and A, then it moves. *F-A-R-M-C-U-T-T-E-R*.

I grimace. That makes no sense. "I don't understand," I say with a shake of my head. "What?" I whimper, near frantic. The dreaded words come out. "Are you her?"

*No.*

I swallow hard. "Is she alive?"

There's a long pause, too long. *Yes.*

I feel the relief wash over me as I sag against the shelf next to me. "Thank God."

The piece is still moving though. *H-U-R-T*. It stops for a long moment.

"Hurt?" I say, trying to make sure I understand it correctly. "What do you mean?"

*P-R-I-S-O-N-E-R*

My stomach tightens, my heart bounds harder and blood rushes to my face. Prisoner? "Where?"

*F-A-R-M*. Pause. *C-U-T-T-E-R*.

I shake my head, frantic. Salt prickles my eyes and I whine at it. "I don't understand. What farm? What cutter?" The tears of desperation start to leak out of my eyes. I can hardly breathe and everything feels like fire. "Where is my sister?" I scream at it.

A moment later, someone comes up behind me. "Syd? What the hell are you doing?" John kneels down beside me and grabs my shoulders. "It's okay, Mr. Lowell. I got her. I'm gonna go now." He puts his phone down. "Come on. Let's get you out of here."

"No!" I wrench myself away.

He grabs after me. "Syd, come on. You need to get some rest."

I shake my head, trying to grab at the Ouija board with trembling fingers. "No! No! I need to see. I have to get the answer!" I screech. The world is spinning.

Rougher than I think I've ever seen him, John grabs my wrists, hauls me to my feet and shakes me hard. "Stop. Stop it!" he hisses in my face.

I sag against the bookshelf, sobbing and clawing at the air. "Please, John. Let me finish."

He stares at me, expression livid. "Why didn't you tell me you were seeing things?"

I bite my tongue ring and avoid his eyes.

"You're sick, Syd. Stressed out. We have to go to a doctor." His fingers leave my wrist and grab my shoulders again. "Sydney."

I'm sick...so sick of being treated like this. Of no one ever believing me. What if what I see is true? What if I'm not crazy? What if I'm really seeing signs? What if that little Ouija board piece is telling us exactly where Mia is this very moment and we're not seeing it because John's too preoccupied with me and my imagined psychosis?

"I'm fine!" I yell at him. "Yes," I admit. "Yes, I'm seeing things. But you know what? I think it's the truth. I think you can see it, too."

John gives me one of those pitying expressions, the kind that people reserve for animals going to the gas chamber. "Look, Syd-"

"No, John," I growl, pushing at him with all my strength so that he has to step backward and grasp me harder to keep his balance. He blinks down at me, startled by my outburst. I grab his shirt and wrench him to the side, hard, making him look down. Then I point at the board. "You look."

Reluctantly, John pulls his eyes away from mine and looks down at the Ouija board. It's still moving. Numbers now. *2-1-4*.

John's eyes widen and his hands slide from my shoulders. His jaw starts to sag in awe.

I take a deep, shaking breath. "Maybe I am crazy, John. But not today," I say, even though my voice is trembling and my mind is spinning in circles. "Today, I'm going to go get my sister."

# Thirty-Four:
# Corey

I sit on a scratchy hotel coverlet, facing Sydney with the Ouija board in between us. John stands, arms crossed, leaning against the wall.

"Is this going to work?" he finally asks.

Sydney flashes him an annoyed glare. He's been questioning the legitimacy of this method of communication since he saw me using the board, even though seeing should be all the proof he needs. Despite that, he purchased the board from the pawn shop and brought Sydney here so no one would see her using it.

Now, in the cheap motel room, the air conditioner buzzing, the shades drawn against passers-by, and the sound of the television blaring over the sound of sex next-door to us, I prepare for my interrogation.

Sydney places her fingers on the end of the cursor in proper Ouija board fashion. She gives an uncertain glance at John. "What should I ask it?"

Sighing heavily, John drops his arms and comes toward the bed. He crawls up and nearly sits on me as he puts his fingertips on the other side of the cursor and says, "Where is Mia?"

I find a place for my own fingers and shove them along, showing them the address. Halfway through John says, "I think it's an address."

Sydney's face brightens. "Oh, that's what those numbers were before!"

I finish the address.

John pulls his fingers away. "That's it then. This is where we need to go." He moves as if to get up off the bed.

Sydney reaches out and grabs his wrist. "Wait a second. I want to ask some more questions."

He shakes her off. "What for? We already know everything we need to know."

She frowns at him. It's obvious that she's disappointed in his lack of enthusiasm. I probably would be, too, if I was him. This is really creepy shit to a normal teen boy. "No, we don't. We don't know anything about what's going on at that address, what kind of situation we're walking into. We could end up getting killed or captured. We need to make a plan."

John stares at her for a long moment, his mouth open in stunned silence.

I smile at them. Wasn't he supposed to be mister careful and she the impulsive one? Strange turn of events.

He drops back onto the bed. "Okay."

Sydney licks her lips and puts her fingers back. "What is at that address?"

I say, *"Farm,"* through the board. Then in the best shorthand, text-speak I can manage—because spelling everything out is obnoxious, *"Cutter. Bad. Blood."*

"Blood?" Sydney chokes, her eyes flashing to John's.

He hunches in, suddenly intent. "What? Is she hurt?"

I slide the cursor to *"yes."* Then at his expression of dismay add, *"A-L-I-V-E."* At least, I hope she's still alive.

Sydney says, "You said prisoner before. Were you talking about Mia?"

"*Yes.*"

"She's being held captive, being hurt by someone? Who?"

"*Cutter.*" Then for good measure, I add, "*Bad. Evil. Killer.*"

Sydney makes a whimpering noise and I add, "*Save Mia.*" Just in case she's starting to get cold feet.

John stares down at the board for a long moment. "How?"

I tell them my plan, which is very simple. "*Noon. Cutter gone. Take Mia. Save.*"

John looks up at Sydney. They stare at each other for a long time before Sydney says, "We should tell the police."

John scoffs. "And say what? 'Oh gee, Officer, we were communing with the spirits last night and they've offered us ample reason to assume that your culprit is this guy Cutter who lives at this address? Oh, by the way, one of us is also a certifiable lunatic.' Fuck, Syd," he says, rising again and turning away from her, "*I* don't even believe this."

Sydney is quiet for a long time and when she speaks, there are tears in her eyes. "I'm not a lunatic."

John lets out a long sigh. "When are you going to admit you have a problem?"

She gnaws her lip. "I've done everything I'm supposed to. Gone to the doctor, taken the meds," she reasons, her voice a whine of frustration.

John rubs his eyes, shoving his hands through his hair. "I know. But it doesn't help our case for the cops. You're not a credible witness. You know that."

She puffs up a little, her eyes fiery. "This isn't my psychosis, John. This is real."

He shakes his head. "I just...this is too weird. Too convenient. I'm gonna wake up...I can't believe it."

"Well I do," Sydney blurts. "Besides, we have no other options, right?" She sits forward. "It's at least worth a try. We're going to at least try, aren't we?" Her expression is so desperate, she looks as though she's going to cry again.

John gives her an acid glare. "Of course I am. I'm just saying that without probable cause, there's nothing to go to the police with."

Sydney hugs herself, goose bumps breaking out on her skin despite the air conditioner's inability to properly cool a room. In the next room, a man groans in ecstasy over the whimpering of his female counterpart. Sydney looks down, hiding behind her curtain of dreads. "We're on our own then."

John slumps down on the other bed. "Yeah. We are."

***

Later that night, when Sydney thinks John is asleep—though I know he's not because no one in their right mind could sleep the night before breaking into a killer's house to save a torture victim—she grabs the Ouija board and tiptoes into the bathroom.

# Thirty-Five:
# Sydney

Placing the Ouija box on the stained bathroom counter, I flip on the vent so that its squealing noise will drown out the sound of my voice. For a long moment, I gaze into my own dark-circled eyes, trying to find the courage I know I have somewhere inside of me. When I look away, I open the box slowly, still half terrified of what I've been experiencing, still half hoping that everything that has happened in the past few days has been a nightmare and I'm going to wake up soon.

But I know it's the truth. My big sister is gone. My parents are even more absent to me than they ever were. I'm on a hair-brained expedition to save Mia—with her ex-boyfriend of all people. And, if John hadn't seen what I saw, I'd have an acute episode of my schizophrenia to add to that lovely list. But seriously? A Ouija board that has a life all its own? That's scary in itself. And what it wants us to do? Even more frightening.

I unfold the board and put it on the cold, white-tiled floor then fold up a towel and sit on it. I stare at the plastic magnifier, too frightened to touch it. But it doesn't wait for me to gather my bravery before it decides it wants to chat some more.

*"Hello, Sydney."*

My stomach sinks and ice coils down to my stomach. "H-how do you know my name?" I demand.

*"I hear."*

Oh yeah, I guess that makes sense. Wait, does it? I'm not sure...is this part real? Am I hallucinating this conversation? I resist the urge to get to my feet and go wake John. "I-I um, I had another question."

When I don't say anything else it says, *"O.K."*

I take a deep breath. I feel really stupid asking this. "Are you real?"

A pause. *Yes.*

Did I expect something else? Of course a hallucination would say it's real. Well, hallucination or no... "Are you—are you good? Like, not a demon? No tricks?"

*"Yes. Good. Try. Help."*

I adjust my seat, trying to find comfort in a drastically uncomfortable situation. "Why are you helping us?"

*"Not want Mia die."*

I frown, a little confused by the short response. "You...you don't want Mia to die?"

*"Yes."*

"I don't understand. Why do you care? Are you like," I struggle for the words, "a guardian angel or something?"

*"No."*

"Then what are you?"

A pause and then the plastic magnifier scratches slowly letter to letter, spelling out, *"Dead."*

I stare at the board for a long moment, trying to digest the word. I suppose it makes sense, Ouija boards are meant to commune with the spirits after all, but this? This is beyond surreal. But this is what I wanted, wasn't it? This is what I wanted to believe existed. I wanted my ghosts to be real, for my hallucinations to be real. And maybe that's why this entity came to me.

"You're a ghost?"

*"Yes."*

For some reason, I all of a sudden know and I understand what's going on. "This Cutter person, they killed you, didn't they? You're trying to save my sister from the same fate."

Another long pause. *"Yes."*

I tuck my hands under my thighs, warming them because I feel so cold. Perhaps it's because I'm sitting in the room with a dead person. That should bother me, but for some reason it doesn't. I feel very secure and I think this ghost does, too. I think it likes being able to talk. "What are you called?"

*"Corey."*

"Corey," I breathe.

*"Rossi."*

I sit up. "Wait, what?" I gasp. "*The* Corey Rossi?"

*"Yes."*

I blink at the cursor, then look around the room, as if expecting to see the boy whose face you couldn't help but remember because he was handsome and lost and everyone cared. "You're dead?" After all that looking? All that hope his parents had? All the hope the whole country had?

He was only a little older than me, had so much more living to do, was loved by so many. Dead. Dead like my sister would have been if not for him finding us.

I look away, needing to not look at him even though he's invisible anyway. But I saw the dead once, who knows when it will come back. "I'm sorry."

He doesn't respond. And why should he? What could he say in response to that? Pity does nothing for the dead.

I shake myself out of it and draw a deep breath. "Thank you. For helping her, for finding us." The words can't be more heartfelt, but even so, I feel I must ask more of him. "Will you stay? Till the end? Help me save her?"

No hesitation. *"Yes."*

And I smile at my new ally.

# Thirty-Six:
# Corey

The drive to the farm is quiet, tense, and a little excited. It's understandable. Both Sydney and John are excited and hopeful that this "try" will result in them finding Mia. They are both putting their faith in a ghost, taking a gamble on something they both logically want to argue against but are trying to have faith in anyway.

John is trying hard to believe—to have faith that Sydney isn't somehow pulling his leg. And Sydney is trying even harder. I can see her terror, her uncertainty in her own sanity. I wish I could not be real for her, wish it didn't have to be her who I decided to reach out to. But perhaps it's because she's a little crazy that she noticed me at all.

I feel guilty I'm putting her through this—making her question her own sanity, and in turn making everyone she loves question her. But I'm not sorry. Because in the end I'll be affirming that everything she's seen because of me is true.

They will find Mia at the farm. However, the condition they find her in will be another story. It's been three days since I left Mia barely clinging to life as it was. She could be much worse off...maybe even dead.

And I'm certain that Sydney and John also know and dread that outcome. We don't know what we'll find when we get into The Room. On top of that fearful apprehension is the foreboding feeling of venturing into the belly of the beast. We will be going to the farm when Cutter is not home, but that doesn't make breaking into a murderer's house any less terrifying in their eyes.

Even I'm apprehensive. The farm isn't someplace I want to be either. It's not a place I want to go back to.

The drive is shorter than expected and we pull off of the main road and onto the long dirt driveway at 11:51 in the morning.

# Thirty-Seven:
# Sydney

John's phone says, "Arriving at destination," and my stomach leaps into my throat. It's hard to breath behind that bloated metaphoric organ in my esophagus. I clench my hands around my purse and my heart suddenly begins pounding and my blood starts to quicken. I lean forward, scanning the dirt driveway as he turns off of the road.

It's slow going, the potholes jostling us and the overgrown brush scratching at the side of the car as John pushes on at less than a mile an hour. The creeping forward is maddening, I want to scream at him to step on it, but suddenly the greying body of a huge farmhouse looms up out of the trees and I bite my tongue.

It's like a horror movie. The kind you expect. Barren, overgrown farmyard full of dirt and rusted, forgotten equipment. Rotten barn, ready to fall down, ready to unload its secret stalls filled with cages and chains. Squat, lumbering farmhouse that seems to both creep up and recede with various turns of the head.

John pulls in beside it, not near the front where the porch looks like it houses booby traps in it's sinking timbers, nor near the side door where a well-worn path through the weeds and long, rutted tire tracks indicate where the murderer prefers to drive, but on the other side of the house, where the lilac bushes are thick and hang on and over the car, sheltering it from sight.

He turns off the ignition and we both sit for a long time. John examines the side of the house, craning his neck as he tries to look through the dirty window. The house was white once, I think, at least the peeling paint seems to say so. It's old...at least from the 20s, possibly older.

John takes a really deep breath and lets it out. "Okay, let's do this."

He gets out, and I follow him.

We both stoop low under the bushes, avoiding branches and bees and spiders. I try not to breathe, but I can smell the area around me anyway.

It smells hot, and dry, and flowery—which I don't like at all. It's like a sick perfume trying to hide the smell of rot. Even though the empty parking space by the screen door indicates that this Cutter guy is not at home, John presses close to the house and inches along, his shoulder scraping off dried paint and green mold as he goes.

Swallowing, I do the same, watching my feet as I go. Twigs, dried leaves, mushrooms. A window to the basement. Something moves inside, making me gasp and jump into John, flat tiring him.

"Fuck, Sydney," he hisses, turning on me. But, upon seeing the terror on my face, he bites his lips together and takes my hand, leading me into the hot summer sun.

We stand at the corner of the house, watching, examining. For what, I don't know.

Everything is still and heavy. It's desolate. I expect a family of inbred cannibals to come crawling out of the hundreds of dark little hidey-holes available in the immediate area. The only place of warmth is a flower garden growing on the sunny side of the barn. A veritable rainbow of bright color and promise. It's probably where the scent is coming from.

For a moment, I want to walk across the dirt yard and slip between the pickets and pipes that enclose it—get lost in the vines and tall stalks and bushes. But then I realize it's probably fertilized with the bodies of the dead and I step closer to John.

"Well?" he asks.

I blink up at him. "Well what?"

He meets my eyes. For once, John looks scared. "You see anything?"

I glance back around. Down the driveway, around the side of the house, out toward the barn, the bracken stricken little pond behind it, the garden, the yard with all it's abandoned equipment and rotted-out cars, the dirt path leading into the woods, and I shake my head. "No."

He takes another deep breath. "Inside?"

I nod. It's most likely where she is. Maybe she was that shadow in the basement? John goes to the screen door and tests the handle. The wooden frame opens on squealing hinges and I can see all the tiny tears that years of use and abuse have punched into the wire mesh.

Holding it open with his body, John tests the inside door. Locked. He looks around the frame, makes a couple of calculations, then nods to himself.

I wipe clammy hands on my shorts and look around again.

"Syd," he whispers, startling me.

I look back and he gestures me over. "Hold this open."

Reaching out, I latch my fingers around the little metal handle on the screen. It's a tiny handle, mottled with tarnish and patina, the ornamental rings worn down with years of handling. I close my eyes against the realization that I'm touching something a killer touched.

But the sensation quickly erases as John suddenly barrels past me and slams bodily into the door. There's a terrible splintering sound as the bolt blasts through the dried and termite-ridden frame and the door swings, slamming against the wall and reverberating back so that it swings halfway closed, hiding John from me.

Almost immediately, a dog starts barking. I go ice and frozen, terrified that I'll suddenly hear thumping paws and the sound of John screaming. But after a minute, nothing happens.

I slide around the screen door and peek around the half-closed inside door. Inside, John is hunched halfway through a kitchen, one hand on a metal-rimmed table, the other on his shoulder. He's staring at a door on the far right-hand side of the room.

Quickly, I glance around. Grungy, dark-wood cabinets on both the right and left sides of the room create a gauntlet of stained and crumb-strewn green counters flanking a table and lone chair.

Cracked, olive green tiles line the floor, making the room look longer and dirtier. There's a paper and a half-finished cup of coffee left on the table. A fly buzzes over the dishes in the two basin sink under the bare window. Beyond the window I can see the top of John's car.

There's an oil-stained stove next to the sink and across from it an old Frigidaire with no magnets. Some kind of ancient floral wallpaper is yellowed and peeling around the wall clock hanging by the entryway into a hall that's dark and ominous.

My eyes flit back to the closed door. It's a basement and the dog is inside of it.

John, seeming to come to the same conclusion, straightens.

I examine the hand on his shoulder. "You all right?"

He nods. "I'll be fine."

I glance around again. "Cheery place."

He sniffs and steps around the table, taking cautious steps toward the hallway. Despite his caution, the floor creeks and the tiles crackle and this just seems to drive the dog below—he must be a friggin big ass dog with that kind of bark—into more of a frenzy.

John glances at the door again, giving it a wide berth as he slips into the hallway. I follow after, reaching out my hands, fingers trailing the cracking wallpaper so that I can keep my balance as I go. The hall is dark, the only promise of light being the strangled bits of sunshine that come from beyond the porch and overgrowth that manage to peek through the blinds.

In front of me, John bumps into something, mutters, "Fuck," and keeps going. I toe forward, finding the little table he must have walked into and inch around it. My fingers find a door, then the handle.

Without thinking, I open it, hoping against hope that there will be light and Mia on the other side. But there is no light and there is no shout of joy from my sister. Instead, it's the distinct smell of mothballs and mildew.

Tentatively, I reach out. My fingers flinch at first, finding something furry, but as my eyes adjust to the low light, I find it's only a closet and close the door.

John's in the adjoining room now, circling around, taking it all in. It's a living room straight out of *A Christmas Story*—minus the stupid leg lamp (instead, the lamps are odd things made out of antlers and deer legs)—and plopped down in *Fargo*. Hunting lodge meets a touch of the forties. I stare up at the mounted deer hanging over my head, then at all the knives lining the walls. Lifeless eyes and deadly weapons. Yet, they all seem to be aiming at me. Cozy.

John seems to feel the same way and quickly moves to the other side of the room. There's another room off of the living room. John examines it, frowns, and takes the stairs instead. I glance into it.

It's a long, bright room with paintings and sculptures. A tall stool sits under a table littered with dried clay, and an easel stands at the far end with a stool before it. Everything is spattered with brownish paint, which seems, more than anything, to just ruin it all. I wrinkle my nose, confused. I'll never get modern art.

I quickly climb the stairs after John, each one creaking and groaning under my weight, making me feel like I'm going to fall through at any moment.

At the top there's another long hall, three doors on each side. All closed, except for the one that John now has opened. He looks inside, then closes it behind him.

"What is it?" I ask.

He doesn't answer. I don't bother to open and look. Instead, I take the one across from it. It opens with a squeak. Master bathroom of some kind, I can tell by the door opening into the other room. I move to close it, but a towel falls off of the ring and flutters toward the other room.

Swallowing, I follow after it.

# Thirty-Eight:
# Corey

Sydney stoops to pick up the towel, but she pauses mid-bend when her eyes find the body in the bed on the other side of the room. At least, it looks like a body. Mia looks dead.

But I know she's not. If she were dead, she'd be gone. Unless, of course, she's died in the time since Cutter left her this morning.

I rush to her side. "How is she?"

Frank looks up at me, eyes sad, and shrugs. He's faded around the edges, as if he's depleting.

"I can't," he says weakly. "I can't do this anymore."

"What?"

He looks into the corner. "Keep watch. I can't watch him...I can't. And them?"

"What?" I demand. "Frank, we have help now!"

He shakes his head. "They keep coming up here. Keep looking. Keep watching her. I can't stand to see them no more."

"You're not making any sense!" I yell.

He glances up, as if seeing me for the first time. "Oh, you're back. You're back." A mad smile plays across his face. "Okay. Okay. If you're back, I'm gonna go now."

"What?!" I growl. "No, no, Frank. Not now. We need to help them—"

But Frank's going, fading. And pretty soon I can't see him. And if a ghost can't see another ghost, I'm pretty sure that means something final.

Panicked, I look back to Sydney, still frozen mid-stoop and still staring. Her expression is wide and wounded. Taking it in, probably. It will take her a full moment to register the horror that her sister has endured. To get past the thick, stained bandages, the odd pajamas, the gaunt face, the sallow skin, the pain and shame and misery. She may be even too afraid to touch Mia for fear she'll dissolve or be cold...dead.

The door to the hall opens and John is suddenly there, too. And he's frozen, but not for nearly as long as Sydney has been. He opens his lips and practically dives across the room. Collapsing at Mia's side, he's touching her face, yelling her name and shaking her. When she doesn't respond, his fingers find her pulse.

Sydney slowly straightens, her expression desperate, her chest heaving and her tears falling. "Is she?"

John's shoulders sag and he collapses into Mia, embracing her frail body and burying his face in her sour scent and ratty hair. I can barely hear him moan, "You're alive."

Sydney takes a step forward, then hesitates. "What do we do? We have to get her out."

John's head snaps up as he takes in the full situation. He stands, his fingers clawing at the cuffs. "We have to get her out of these! Find the key, or something to cut them. A tool box. I'll look up here, you go downstairs and look."

Sydney stays frozen for a moment, just staring.

John growls at her as he gets to his feet, "Go!"

Spurred into action, Sydney stumbles out of the room, taking the hall at a run and practically falls down the stairs, which gets Delilah barking up a new frenzy. Panicked at the bottom of the stairs, Sydney casts about, her eyes searching and her breath heaving. "Tools. Tools. Fuck, where are the tools?!"

Her brain seems to function then and she pounds back through the hall and skids to a stop in front of the basement door.

"No!" I yell at her. "Not there!"

But she doesn't hear. Sydney throws the bolt on the door and wrenches it open, the stench from below like a wave of carrion. As Sydney gasps and throws her hands over her nose and mouth, Delilah suddenly falls eerily silent. In the dark, I can almost see her expectant eyes gleaming in the darkness.

Sydney lowers trembling fingers and peers into the impenetrable darkness. "N-nice doggy."

She steps closer, standing at the edge of the precipice. I can hear Delilah breathing down below, like a bellows. Her too-long claws click on the cement floor as she circles under Sydney. Swallowing hard, Sydney reaches out and probes the sides of the wall just inside of the door, looking for a switch. When she finds nothing, she reaches out and above her, looking for a pull cord.

When she finds nothing, she rocks back on her heels and stares into the dark.

John calls from upstairs, "Anything yet?"

"No!" she replies. She turns her attention back to the door. "You can do this, Syd. You've always liked animals and they've always liked you. See, he's probably just standing there waiting for you to pet him."

"No, you twit. Not down there!" Frustrated, I cast about in search of anything to tell her otherwise.

# Thirty-Nine:
# Sydney

I'm taking a step forward when suddenly something shatters behind me, startling me into losing my balance. I throw out my hands and catch myself just as my foot realizes that it's so black down that stairwell because there *is* no stairwell. Panting, I pull myself back into the room. The dog down below is barking again, his feet clicking in a tight circle directly under me.

Okay, maybe not the basement.

Then where?

I examine the kitchen. The coffee mug has fallen off the table, shattering and exploding its contents on the floor.

"Corey?" I whimper.

The coffee on the floor begins to streamer out from the main puddle in long lines. B-A-R-N.

"Oh," I breathe, stunned by my own stupidity to realize that sooner.

In a flash, I'm slamming my hands against the screen door and running across the yard in a blinding haze of sunlight. It takes a couple of attempts to kick and push and pull the sliding barn door open enough to slip through and even more precious minutes of standing in brilliant white spots to get my eyes to readjust to the dark.

Inside the barn, the light streams through the slats, illuminating dust motes. The dirt aisle is wide with stalls and closed-in little rooms on either side and a yawning loft above. Hanging on the beams are dozens of odd tools and pieces of equipment that look more like they belong at a slaughter house.

Shuddering, I creep out from under them. In front of me, there's a white van that just screams 'child molester' and I get the feeling that's exactly what it is. I give it a wide berth, checking in stalls as I go. Stacks of old blankets, bales of moldy hay, rat-chewed sacks of sawdust and feed, dried-out pieces of tack.

In one of the stalls, I find what I'm looking for. Two giant tool boxes, a work bench, and more handheld tools than I can identify. It makes Nick's dad's little collection in their garage look pitiful.

I rummage in a couple of drawers until I find what I hope are bolt cutters. Hefting the bolt cutters, I trot back toward the house...and stop dead in my tracks.

On the other side of the yard, a man that might as well be goliath is getting out of a beat up old Chevy pick-up. I shrink back into the darkness of the barn, breathing hard.

"Shit," I whisper. I thought Cutter was supposed to be gone? Well, apparently not.

I peek around the corner, watching him as he walks up the path, whistling, and gets to the door. He immediately notices something is wrong. He opens the screen door, examines the broken frame with his fingers, then pulling his cap down low over his hidden features, he sets his bulging shoulders and slips into the house.

Oh no...John!

Heart hammering and mouth dry as the dust in the yard, I slide out of the barn and scamper to the edge of the house. I peek around the corner and through the screen door. Cutter is standing in the kitchen, surveying the mess. The spilled coffee, the wide open basement door. He glances down at the barking dog and his displeased expression alone elicits a yelp and obedient silence from the beast below.

Footsteps above draw his glance and for the first time I see Cutter's face. He's not an attractive person, by any measure, but he's certainly not in possession of any of the kind of monstrous traits you assume murderers have. He just looks like an average Joe.

But of course, he's not. I tighten my grasp on the bolt cutters. Not by far. He's the monster who kidnapped my sister, kept her prisoner, tortured her, and did I-don't-even-want-to-know what else to her.

Hate seethes through me and an overwhelming urge to bash his brains in overpowers me, making me leap out and expose myself in the frame of the screen door. But Cutter has already turned away and is heading toward the stairs. Toward John. And Mia.

No. We've come too close to fail now.

And in that moment, I know I will incapacitate Cutter, or die trying. Because I can't let him keep Mia. I can't let him do to John and me what he did to Mia.

Taking a slow breath, I put my hand on the screen door handle and let myself in as silently as the squeaky hinges will allow and tiptoe after Cutter.

# Forty:
# Corey

If I were a real person, I'd be suffocating Sydney. I cling to her as she inches through the broken glass in the kitchen, slides along the wall to avoid her shadow attracting Delilah's attention, and disappears into the darkness of the hall.

Cutter's feet are almost soundless as they pass on the stairs above and to our right. We follow after, soundless as snakes, Sydney surprisingly remembering exactly which steps to avoid so that her pursuit of Cutter isn't announced by a loose nail.

When we get to the landing, Cutter is peeking into rooms. He opens the door to his room and stares in, long and hard.

John's voice emerges, muffled, and I assume he must be inside Cutter's walk-in closet. "Is that you, Syd?"

Cutter doesn't reply.

"Have you found anything? I've got nothing. You'd think he'd hide the key in here."

Cutter's fingers fly unconsciously to his neck. Sydney doesn't miss the gesture. Cutter slides out of sight, going into the room. Sydney and I follow, stopping just outside the door, watching from the hall as Cutter creeps up on John. And just as he's upon John, John must hear him or see his reflection on something in the closet because he ducks at the last minute.

Cutter, having put his weight into his attack, stumbles forward into the closet, crashing into a rack of clothes with an *oomph*. John scuttles under his outstretched arms, throws the door half-closed behind him, and leaps across the bed, landing in a tuck and roll then coming up in an Olympian finish. He springs to his feet, launches toward the far wall and spins around, ready to face Cutter who, howling, twists around and lurches after him.

Only John did a really good job of pulling Cutter's closet apart and Cutter trips over an old photo box and face-plants into the bed.

John takes the moment to try and rush past, but Cutter recovers quickly, lunging again, and his big hands catch at John's leg and trip him up. John goes down hard, landing almost on top of Sydney, who shrinks back, but he twists and kicks at Cutter, who lets go. John does a hasty crab-walk the remainder of the way out of the room, Cutter in his own hasty crawl, hot on his heels.

John hits the wall, eyes wide, blood pouring out his nose. Cutter leaps at him and grabs his neck between his two big paws.

And then Sydney is suddenly between them and me, her arms raised high. The bolt cutters come down hard and make a horrible *thunk*ing noise as they come into contact with Cutter's head.

For a moment, they're all frozen. And then Cutter slowly slumps and John begins kicking and punching his way free of Cutter's limbs. He finds his feet, huffing. He looks down at Cutter who is lying on the floor, blood gushing out of his head, and then at Sydney.

Suddenly seeming to realize what she has done, Sydney drops the bolt cutters and scrubs her shaking hands on her stomach. Then she darts in, grabs at the key around Cutter's neck and yanks the chain loose.

John and I both stand stupid as she skitters back into The Room. She's already trying to get the key into the cuffs when John and I finally shake ourselves out of it and rejoin her. The key slips out of her hand and lands on the floor. She picks it up and tries again, but her hands are shaking too bad. John steps forward, his hands folding over hers and helping to guide the key to her sister's release.

In just a few moments, Mia Lowell is free of her bonds. John lifts her into his arms like a proper knight and kisses her forehead. As if on her fairy-tale cue, Mia's eyes flitter open. Groggy and empty.

Sydney steps forward and takes her hand. "Mia?" She stares into Mia's vacant gaze and then at John. "She doesn't look good. We should call an ambulance."

John nods. "Let's get her out of here first."

Sydney and I trail after him, both anxious but excited, too. In moments, they'll be driving off into the sunset and I will have saved someone from my killer's clutches.

They get to the living room where John sets Mia down on a musty, moth-eaten chair and finally takes a moment to scrub his hand under his nose, smearing the blood across his lip. "Okay, I'll call an ambulance and then we'll wait outside." He reaches into his pocket, pulls out his phone, and then grimaces.

A shadow crosses over Sydney's face. "What?"

"There's no signal."

Sydney slumps her shoulders. "Oh, come on!"

John holds up the phone and spins in a slow circle. "Probably outside. Stay with her, I'll be back in a minute."

"But—" Sydney is arguing, but John's already in the kitchen.

# Forty-One:
# Sydney

As the screen closes with a smack behind John, I hunch into myself and glance around, still uneasy. "He could have at least brought her outside," I mutter.

I stare down at Mia, who's slumped like a forgotten and weather-beaten little ragdoll on the chair. God, just look at her. Look what's he's done to her. "I don't feel bad for killing him," I tell her, wiping at my eyes. "Not at all."

Mia's lips are moving, the peels and sores exaggerating the tiny movements she's managing. I kneel down beside her, trying to understand. "What?"

"Wha, wha," Mia is rasping, her eyes staring upward.

"Water?" I wonder. "Okay. Okay, I'll get you some water." I get to my feet and head toward the kitchen. I try one cabinet and then another, frantic and annoyed that Cutter couldn't use a normal person's layout for his kitchen. I leave door after door open until I finally find a glass. I fill it up in the sink, not bothering to turn it off all the way, and run back to Mia.

I practically fall on top of her and spill half of the water in my attempt to get it to her as quickly as possible.

"Here. Water. Dri—" Something snatches me from behind and hauls me high and wide. I feel the earth leave my feet and the glass leave my hands, feel the air take me into her arms and gravity snatch back at me as the huge body of Cutter summersaults round and about with the stuffed fish on his walls. I land hard, the wind going out of me and my bones feeling like they've all snapped. For a moment, it's as if I stick there and then gravity wins against air and I slide to the floor, taking with me a couple of knife display cases that crash about me so that I land in glass and cold metal.

I can't move; I blink stars. More heavy hands. Cutter hands. I force myself to move, to kick and punch and squirm despite the glass and knives.

All I see are flashes: the 49 on his hat, a chin, my hands, the flash of silver. All I feel is pain, sharp and blunt, hands and glass. And the air in my lungs. And the beating of my heart. And my bleating calls.

A bellow sounds and suddenly there's a flash of white.

The onslaught disappears for an instant, long enough for me to blink my vision clean. John's on Cutter's back, his arms wrapped around his neck. Cutter is spinning, bucking and braying like a bronco. I struggle to my feet, my fingers finding a blade in the glass as my hands lever me up.

John flies away and Cutter spins around, seeing me standing there with a knife. And then it's like a bull and his red cape. He charges and I backpedal, slashing and screaming as I go.

I back into the kitchen, into the table. And then there is nowhere to go before he's on me. Hands are grabbing at the knife like he doesn't care about its slashing bite. I feel it bite into him, feel the blood on my fingers. But I can't look away from those dark, emotionless eyes, wreathed in blood. His fingers steal away the knife. His body bears against me, heavy, suffocating. I punch him. Nothing. He's a brick wall, a house. But he punishes me anyway, grabbing my hair and slamming my head against the table. Once. Twice. Then he drags me up and slams my body hard against the counter.

My feet go out from under me and I collapse, my body incapable of standing because my brain can't seem to figure out which way is up. I can't see straight. There's this horrible ringing in my ears.

He has the knife now and is standing over me with a horrible leer that is too perfect on his face to be something ill practiced. I blink up at him, wobbling, uncertain. My ears pop and suddenly I can hear again. The dog is barking more ferociously than ever.

"Do you desire my blades, too?" he asks me.

I open my mouth. To plead, to scream, to curse him and his mother? I don't know what. Whatever I'm going to say, it doesn't come.

"Hey," the voice is an ugly rasp against my eardrums.

Cutter turns and over his shoulder, we're both surprised to see Mia wavering on her feet. Cutter pulls away from me and backs up to keep us both in his line of sight.

"Little Duck," he says, adding a nasty *tsk*ing of his tongue. "You should be in bed."

Mia seems to lose a little of her strength, slumps against the doorway, but she rights herself and steps into the room, using the counter as balance. Her eyes never leave Cutter. "Leave my sister alone." Her voice is like tearing paper and something from the grave.

Cutter smiles at her, humoring her. "How are you even walking, Little Duck?"

A grin plays at Mia's features, it's a hollow and ghastly thing that speaks too much of the horrors she has seen. "You don't want to know."

He cocks his head.

"They give me strength, you know? Helped me stay alive. I didn't know what they wanted at first, but..." Mia lifts her hand and makes a fist. "I know now."

Somehow, though I don't understand how, I feel someone touch my back. A voice whispers in my ear, "Let me help you."

Startled, I glance over my shoulder, but there is no one there. Despite that, I feel him there. Corey. He's pushing at me, almost like an urging. I feel his strength against my skin, empowering me, giving me strength.

Part of me rejects it, tells me not to let him in, not to accept his help, because that would be a true fold to my insanity. But it's life or death... Not just my life, but Mia's and John's, too. I'd embrace any hallucination for that.

Swallowing, I cast about, searching for something—anything to help me. My eyes fall on the broken mug on the floor.

Mia is still moving forward. Cutter is still beside me, unmoving, but tense with suspicion.

I reach out and, with Corey's strength to help me, I pick up the bottom of the mug. And then, I slash at Cutter's tendon.

For the third time in one day, I experience what it's like to damage another person's body. It's a terrible thing. The way the skin breaks and the blood comes. The way the parts inside tear and give way. But, like when I hit him over the head and when I cut him with the blade, I have no remorse or mercy for Cutter. Because now, with Corey somehow sitting inside my body, I see his mind, see his memories.

I know what it was like to be beaten and bound, to be tortured with knives, to be forcefully castrated, to be skinned alive. And if I could hold Cutter down and cut him up just like he cut up his victims, I would. But unfortunately that's not to be because Cutter spins out of my reach, preventing me from doing more.

He stumbles, his one leg threatening to collapse out from under him, but he regains himself and spins back toward me. And then he laughs. "You'll have to do better than that, Little Sister! I'm a god!"

"Fuck that!" And out of nowhere and with a strength I didn't know someone in her condition could possess, Mia explodes away from the counter, barrels into him, and they both go tumbling toward the open maw of the basement. Mia releases him at just the last moment, landing safely on one side while his body slides over the other.

Cutter howls, his limbs flailing, catching at the door jamb. Down below the hound whips into a frenzy, and Cutter starts screaming as his body is wrenched this way and that. I can only imagine that the dog has grabbed onto his leg and is already halfway through digesting him.

I look on, horror struck as Mia, face contorted somewhere between an avenging angel's and a villain's, kicks at his face and stomps his hands until it seems he's going to let go. And then, in some burst of fight and flight adrenaline, he grabs onto her leg as the hound finally pulls him.

As she falls, Corey takes utter control and dive bombs after her, catching her fingers.

For a long moment we dangle into the darkness before he—using strength I don't possess because I can't even do a pull up in gym—pulls us back into the kitchen and shoves the door shut.

Heaving, we both sit on the other side of the door as we listen to Cutter get eaten alive by his hellhound. When he falls silent, when the sirens start to sound in the distance, we finally look into each other's eyes and smile. Corey props Mia up, slides away from me, and stands. For the first time, I see him.

Tall and muscular, looking just as lovely as those photos they showed of him on TV, he stares down at Mia. "I thought you weren't going to help me."

Mia looks back up at him, her expression maniacal and self-satisfied. "We didn't help you. We helped her. She asked, we couldn't say no."

Corey lowers his chin. "I'm glad. It's all over now. You can go now."

And just like that, they start seeping out of Mia. One, after another, after another. Five more ghosts, kids...and one older man. Until all that's left is an unconscious girl who slumps against me.

"Mia!" I cry, grasping at her. I look up, desperate. "Is she...?"

Corey smiles at me. "She's okay." His eyes flash over the ghosts who are standing there with him. "We all are, I think. It's nice to see you, Frank."

The older man nods, then fades. As the sirens come into the yard, they all fade away, leaving only Corey who looks down at me. "Take care of her, okay?"

"Wait, but—"

The door bursts open and suddenly there are more people than I can count. Police and EMTs and firemen. Someone hauls me up, takes Mia from my arms. I try to fight them, try to stop them. I don't want to leave Mia, not ever again...but then they inject me with something and everything just kind of fades.

# Forty-Two:
# Mia

It's John's voice that I hear first. He sounds like he's having a one-sided conversation with himself. I listen to his smooth baritone, let it drag me up between dreaming and dead, let him warm me into reality and my body.

His voice. Calm and certain as always.

Ti's voice. High and sobbing. She's crying. Why is she crying?

My breathing, slow, shallow.

My arms and legs, wrapped and warm. Everything is warm and heavy.

I can't move, can't lift my head. I can't open my eyes. Too heavy.

I'm paralyzed! A second later, panic kicks in and I hear frantic beeping. Something in my hand tightens. Another hand, wrapped in mine. And then another one in the other hand.

"Shhhh," I hear John say. His fingers slide through my hair. "It's okay, babe, I got you. I got you." He presses his hand against my cheek.

"Joh—" I cry out, but it's only a squeak.

His fingers press against my lips, his callused skin against the dry and cracked roughness. "Shhh."

I feel desperate, stinging tears leak out of my eyes. I'm paralyzed! I'm broken! Where am I? What's going on?

I sense breath on my face and a moment later, I feel John's lips on mine. It has been so long. So long since I felt that kiss. A kiss that has always sent tingles all the way to the tips of my toes. And still does. Not paralyzed then.

John trails kisses across my face, wipes the tears away with the pads of his thumbs. I calm a little bit, certain it can't all be too bad if he's here.

The person holding my other hand squeezes harder. I try to open my eyes again. The world spins around and my eyes instantly want to shut again. I feel like I have weights on me dragging me into sleep, but I fight against them, struggling for consciousness.

I catch John, swing my attention to the other side and see Ti, tense and anxious. I try to smile for both of them. The two people I love and want to see most, right here with me. I must be in heaven. The weights finally win and I fall back into the void.

***

Some time later, hours or days—when the medicine wears off enough for me to understand that I'm in a hospital, I sit in my hospital bed and watch TV with everyone who is the most important to me. John lies in the bed beside me, Ti sits on the other side, her hand never leaving mine. My parents are sitting on either side of my sister.

Dad doesn't have his laptop, Mom's in jeans and a hoodie. Sydney is holding both their hands and grinning like an idiot.

They're watching the news—which is talking about Cutter. I try not to listen, instead trying to distract Ti into a conversation.

"So, what did you tell your mom about the party?" I ask.

She drags her eyes away from the television and gives me a sad smile. I can tell she'd rather not talk about it. There's this awkwardness about us now, a walking on glass and lack of trust. It's going to take a while to get over, but it's not insurmountable. She's here now, being a friend to me now, and that's what matters.

I squeeze her hand. "Ti, it's okay." I smile, trying to encourage her. "We're good." I glance at John for emphasis. He's not paying attention, he's looking at the TV.

Ti bites her lip and tears fill her eyes. "I'm so sorry," she whimpers.

"You should be," I hear Sydney say.

"Hush, Syd," my mom says. Then, suddenly brightened by some marvelous idea, she pounces to her feet. "I know, why don't you, me, and Dad go get some ice cream?"

Sydney blinks up at her, her expression confused.

I smile. Looks like she's finally getting her wish.

"But," Syd says, turning her attention to me. "What about Mia?"

Mom smiles as she tugs on Sydney's hand. "We can bring some back. Vanilla okay with you, Ti?"

Tiana shakes her head. "I have to get home soon."

"Aw darn. Well, coffee for you two?" Mom looks at me and John. I smile as I feel him nod.

My family shuffles out, leaving me with Ti and John. John slips off the bed. "I'm gonna go stretch my legs." He leans over, catches my chin with his finger and kisses me for longer than necessary, but I don't give a crap. I'd kiss him all day. Why did I ever break up with him in the first place?

I watch John leave the room, marveling at his perfect backside until the door closes behind him. Then I turn back to Ti, who promptly bursts out crying and throws herself at me, tossing her arms around me and squeezing the life out of me.

"I'm so sorry!" she wails. "I'm sorry about everything! About telling you to break up with John and Will and making you get abducted! It's all my fault! I've made your life so miserable!"

Unable to comprehend half of what she's saying, I just hug her back as best as I can. It hurts, the cuts on my arms are still pretty fresh, but I do my best. "Ti, it's okay."

She shakes her head against my shoulder. "No, it's not. It's not okay, Mia."

I sigh, uncertain what to say to her. The news pops back to my attention.

"—reports are showing evidence relating to at least two dozen missing persons reports across New England—all of them children. Among those cases is the high profile case of Corey Rossi, a Connecticut high school senior whose father, Gabriel Rossi, staged a multimillion-dollar nationwide search when his son went missing in December of last year."

I let the news float away, thinking of Corey. I hope he's okay. I hope that he's finally found peace. They know where his body is now, know who killed him, and proper justice has been wrought upon his murderer.

"—animal rights activists are speaking out against what they consider an act of animal cruelty toward what many are calling Gabriel's Hound. Danielle Hunter is on the scene."

"Thanks, Lisa. I'm here with Micky Falone, president of the Berkshire Animal Rights Group. Micky, can you tell me what's going on here?"

"I sure can. We're all here to support Gabriel's Hound, the dog who saved the lives of innocent people. We're speaking out against the tyranny of the Berkshire Humane Society. They don't know how to treat a hero. That dog should have been allowed to be rehabilitated and adopted."

I glance up in time to see the screen switch back to Lisa, who reads a quote from the president of the Humane Society. "We did everything in our power to safely remove the dog from the premises. However, you have to keep in mind that when an animal is mistreated to the extent that Howley's dog was, they're often not capable of rehabilitation. We also have to keep in mind that, whether Wayne Howley was a murderer or not, the dog killed a human being and attacked the animal control officers sent to retrieve it. The dog was vicious." She is quiet for a split second. "The Humane Society also tells us that Howley's dog was so sick that it would have more than likely died shortly after capture anyway."

Ti has quieted her tears and tips her head, paying attention to the screen. "Those people make a giant show out of everything."

I pet her hair. "It's a big case."

Her eyes slide toward the window. "They're out there, you know. Waiting to jump on you."

I sigh. "Yeah, I figured as much."

She looks up at me, her eyes searching mine. I reach out and cup her face with my hands. "Ti, seriously, stop looking at me like that. It's not your fault."

She tries to break my gaze, but I jerk her head back. "You're gonna stay dating Will, right?"

Her cheeks flush under my palms. "How'd you know we were dating?"

I smirk. "John told me." I let my hands slide away. "We're back together now. I shouldn't have broken up with him in the first place."

She nods. "I'm sorry about that, too. I shouldn't have encouraged you to break up with him. I was just so jealous. You guys were so perfect and I had no one."

I cock my head. "Well, now we both have someone, right? And we're still best friends, too, right? Because I don't think I'll ever find someone to braid my hair like you do."

She smiles and hugs me again. "I gotta go."

We say our goodbyes and as she's leaving, John slips back into the room. He makes sure the door is shut before slinking over to the bed and sliding under the blankets with me. I snuggle in with him, which is harder than it seems considering my bruised ribs and wrapped limbs. When we're settled, we just stare at each other for a long, long time. Him smoothing my hair with his knuckles, me tracing hearts on his chest.

After a long moment, his hand stops and finds my arm, his eyes wandering toward the bandages.

I avoid looking, too. "The doctors say the scarring will be permanent."

"I know," he whispers.

I curl my fingers into a fist against his chest. Scarred for life. Not just physically but emotionally, too. Already I'm having nightmares, can't stand to be left by myself, jump every time the door opens. Already, they're giving me meds, having me talk to a shrink. PTSD they say, and it's only going to get worse as the shock of it wears off. He doesn't deserve the mess I am, not my beautiful perfect John. "I'm not going to be the same person. Not ever."

He leans closer, presses his forehead against mine and meets my uncertain eyes. "You're changed. I know. But you'll still be my Mia. Nothing can ever change that. God," he whispers, voice choked with emotion. He closes his eyes and shakes his head. "I almost lost you."

I close my eyes, too, and press back against his forehead. "Never again, John. I'm going to stay right here with you." So long as he'll keep me.

His fingers slide through my hair and curl around my neck. "I love you."

I grasp my necklace. My Tiffany heart with Mia engraved on it. "I love you, too." I feel tears of stupidity and relief and love burn against my eyelids. "I'm so sorry," I sob. And the tears start falling.

John pulls me tighter and kisses away my tears.

He holds me and kisses me until I fall asleep.

And he's there when I wake up.

And the day after and the day after.

He holds me close when I wake up screaming at night. He's on the other side of the door when I'm crying in the shower. He offers his shoulder when I'm exhausted from interviews. His hand slides into mine when I'm being stared at on the street.

And it's because he's there that I stay there—forcing myself to stand and fight rather than run. And it's because he loves me despite the ugliness that I learn to also love me, despite the ugliness.

# Forty-Three:
# Mia

I turn off the ignition and stare out over the overgrown lawn. Even though it's late autumn, it's hot and still. It reminds me of the days I spent here.

I close my eyes and take a deep breath, willing myself to keep my cool.

The leaves are heavy orange-gold and the dirt driveway has deep gouges in it. I examine Cutter's house out of the corner of my eye, not wanting to look at it fully. I don't have good memories of this place.

There's still police tape all over—up around the barn and along the porch. It's sagging and detached in some places, a bit faded from the sun, but no one has bothered to pull it down.

It's still a crime scene, isn't it? Even though they gave up dragging cadaver dogs across the property. Even though they've collected what little remains they could from the basement and taken Corey's skin off the wall in Mrs. Howley's bedroom. Even though they've been gone for months, it's still the scene of atrocious crimes.

Sydney shifts next to me and puts her hands on mine, her fingers slipping over my scars. I try not to pull away at the touch, try not to be self conscious about them. I try to look at them like a badge of honor— something I can say I lived through like a soldier might look at a stump or a bullet wound. But I'm no soldier. "Are you sure you want to do this?" she asks.

I give her a tight nod. I don't want to do this. But I *have* to do this. I have to face the ghosts, in more than one way. Before I can convince myself to turn around and speed away, I unbuckle myself and get out of the car.

# Forty-Four:
# Sydney

I get out after Mia. "Wait for me!"

Fueled by some inner strength that I marvel at, she storms across the driveway, tripping and stumbling over the thick grooves that all the police and press vehicles gouged in the driveway. She makes it to the back door and rips the caution tape down. Her hand lashes out and grabs at the screen door handle, and then she goes still.

"What?" I breathe, winded even though I haven't done anything. "What's wrong?"

Mia's fingers tense on the handle. "I can do this, right?" she asks, her voice low and her eyes fixed on the door beyond the screen. She's having a moment of weakness. I'm still not used to these moments, but they come constantly now. She was always brave, always strong. Now...she tries, but it's obviously much harder than it ever was. And I can't blame her.

Now it's my turn to be the strong one. Now it's my turn to prove there are no monsters under the bed.

I reach out and put my hand over hers, reassuring her. "Yes. You can."

She swallows hard, nods and her hand turns the handle. The screen door creaks open. The door itself is partially ajar. It's still broken from when John broke in, no one has bothered to fix it. Mia's hand releases the handle, propping the screen door with one of her scarred legs as she grabs hold of my fingers.

She takes a deep breath, squares her shoulders and pushes the inside door open with her free hand. I don't want to follow Mia into this hell hole. But if she can do it, despite her shaking and everything that happened to her, I have no right to chicken out. I told her I'd be the one to come with her. Not John. Not Ti. Me. I'm the one she asked. And that means something really important.

Clenching my teeth hard, I follow after Mia as she steps back into Cutter's torture house.

The screen door slams behind us as we stand frozen in Cutter's kitchen. It's just as creepy and scary as I remember it. Old and decrepit, the colors washed out and grey, everything dated. The furniture has been overturned or destroyed. The windows have been broken out so that leaves and dirt have blown in to gather in the corners. There are rat droppings all over the counter, dead bugs on the window sills. Dirty dishes are still in the sink.

The door down to the basement has been hastily nailed shut and boarded up. Vandals have been here, scrawling their satanic symbols and names on the walls, writing messages for the unwary that this place is evil. The floor is littered with glass, old food packages, condoms, and beer bottles.

It disgusts me that this place has become a place where assholes come to party, like it's some kind of secret club house. This is a murder house. Dozens of people were tortured and killed here. I feel Mia's fingers tense around mine, tighter and tighter, until I feel like my circulation is going to be cut off.

Mia says, "Looks like we're not the first ones to come here." A breathy little laugh escapes her. "Bet they thought they were *so* brave."

I shake my head even though she can't see it. I don't have words, only stiffness and fear and sickness that other people take pleasure in things like this. Treating a place that was hell to someone I love like it's a funhouse at a carnival, debasing it and making it something less than what it is. It would be like putting on a comedy show in Auschwitz.

Her fingers abruptly pry away from mine and she drops my hand, her voice turning steely. "I'm going to look around."

I let her go, letting her make slow advancing steps across the cracked tiles of the kitchen. She gets to the doorway and stands there for a long moment, bracing herself against the wood. She stares at the wood for a long time, at the notches cut into it. Growth lines. Perhaps cut there by Howley's mother twenty some-odd years ago. She traces the lines with her fingers. "You raised a killer," she whispers. "Do you know that?"

After a long moment, she glances back at me, eyes huge in the low light inside the house. My heart is hammering and I feel sweat dripping down my spine. I want to go outside; I want to escape. I feel things prickling along my spine. Everything about this place cries wrongness, like spiders and cockroaches crawling under my skin. There are ghosts here, and not the kind that possessed my body.

She forces a tentative smile. "It will be okay, Sydney. Just stay here."

Part of me wants to laugh at her. Still being the big sister, still being braver than me. I should be the one comforting her, but the reality is that, even now, she's stronger than I'll ever be.

Mia wakes up screaming bloody murder in the middle of the night, but come morning she's bright and sunny like nothing ever happened. Her limbs are scarred with twists and whorls, like she's endured some kind of tribal scarification ritual, but she doesn't hide them under short sleeves or pants. People stare at her with pity and ask uncomfortable questions, but she ignores them and on good days she actually tells them about it.

She's carrying on, being brave, despite what lurks in the dark recesses of her mind. She's a tried and true survivor. If she can live through Cutter, she can live through anything. I will never hope to understand how she sees the world now, how she even gets out of bed in the morning...or why she has to come back here. And I don't need to. I just have to be there for her when she needs me.

I try my best to smile back at her, encouraging her. She turns around and steps into the darkness. I follow her to the doorway, afraid of losing her again. Mia inches into the darkness of the hall, halting at every creak and whisper. I can hear her breathing hard. I see her step into the grey light of the living room beyond, weaving between two broken chairs.

Everything of value has been taken from the house. The knives and the hunting trophies that were on the wall and some of the other furniture. I guess it didn't matter to the looters that everything in this house is haunted—tainted. She gets to the base of the stairs, puts her hand on the railing and stops.

She looks back at me suddenly. "I can't go the rest of the way."

Thank God. "That's okay, Mia. You don't have to." I don't want her to go up there. I see no reason to ever have to go back into that room.

She pulls her hand away from the railing and takes a few steps back, her hand cradled to her chest. Slowly, Mia turns around, her eyes examining everything. And suddenly, she calls out, "Corey!"

The air whooshes out of my lungs. So that's why she came. Panic claws at me. I've made myself forget about Corey. We don't talk about him...I refuse. I won't talk to anyone about him.

"Corey Rossi!" she calls again.

The silence that follows her voice is maddening. Dread pools in my stomach, a reality that he isn't—was never—a real thing. She spins again, going to the foot of the stairs. "Corey! It's Mia!" Another few moments of silence. Mia puts her foot on the first step and cranes her neck, trying to peer up the stairs. "Corey!"

Somehow feeling like this should be private for Mia and Corey, I back away from the doorway and turn back into the kitchen. For an instant, the dark figure standing by the door makes my stomach explode into my throat. I slap my hand over my mouth to keep from screaming, but then I come to my senses and lower my hand.

It's Corey. His hands and the knees of his jeans are covered in dirt and he's sweaty. He smiles at me, but it doesn't reach his eyes.

I open my mouth to call to Mia, but he lifts his hand and puts a finger over his lips, indicating silence. Confused, I close my mouth and knit my brows at him. We stare at each other for long moments, Mia calling out to him all the while. A moment later, his attention is pulled away from me as Mia's footsteps approach from behind me.

I turn and meet her gaze. She's smiling, her eyes bright and happy. I think this is the happiest I've seen her since before her abduction. "He's not here," she says, excitedly.

I frown at her, glancing back at Corey. He's standing plain as day less than ten feet away from her. He's too big and dark and Greek statue-looking not to notice. I look back at her. "You're sure? You don't see him at all?"

She shakes her head, her grin breaking open and a breath of a laugh escaping. There are tears in her eyes. "You know what that means?"

I shake my head, utterly confused and uncertain of my own sanity.

"It means he's moved on, Syd. He's in heaven now." She crying now. Tears of absolute joy.

Whipping around, I squint at Corey. He doesn't look away from Mia, his expression warm and intimate in the same kind of way that John looks at her when she doesn't know he's looking. Mia comes up behind me and wraps her arms around my shoulders. I don't look away from Corey, he doesn't look away from Mia. She slips away, her arms dragging as if finally able to relax, and she walks past me.

Corey's dark eyes follow her as she walks right up to him, walks right through him, and follow her still as she walks out the door and heads back toward the car.

I step up beside him, watching her as she opens the trunk of her car. "I don't understand," I say. "Can't she see you?"

Corey takes a deep breath. "No."

"Why?"

"I don't want her to."

I glance up at him. "You can control that?"

He shrugs.

I knit my brows, confused as his expression. "You don't want to talk to her?"

His eyes finally turn to me. "Very much. But I love her too much for that, you know? I don't want her to know she can see me. Not yet. She'll figure it out eventually, everyone touched by death eventually does, right?"

I look away, uncertain how to take the news. "So she's gonna be like me? She's gonna think she's crazy?"

He's quiet for a long time. "I don't think she'll look at it like that."

"But it's the truth." I look away, unable to hold eye contact with him. "Now we're both crazy." The realization that I'm no longer alone doesn't bring me comfort. Mia's had enough, she doesn't deserve this.

Corey's eyes tighten in thought. "What you have is a gift, Sydney. Maybe you should actually think about it like that."

Scowling, I look away. A gift? No, no, this is a curse. Isn't it? I glance back up at Corey, then away again. I'm so confused. "So you haven't moved on?"

Out of the corner of my eye, he shakes his head. "Apparently not. She doesn't need to know that though. Don't ever tell her."

I close my eyes and lower my chin. "You see what she's doing, don't you?"

"Yes."

I open my eyes. "What's going to happen to you?"

"I don't know."

A long moment passes as we continue to watch Mia. Finally, I say, "Thank you. For helping my sister."

I feel a solid hand touch my shoulder. "Thank you for avenging my murder."

I look up at him, finally able to meet his eyes, and I smile at him.

A moment later, Mia comes back in, both her hands full. "Ready?"

Corey's fingers slide away from my shoulder and he steps back, fading into the wall. I watch after him.

"Syd?"

I glance back at Mia. Her eyes are so bright, so expectant. I smile at her and I nod.

# Forty-Five:
# Mia

I splash the last of it on the stairs, wanting to make sure to create a path all the way to the top. To The Room. Taking a deep breath that stings my lungs and my nose, I let it out and glance around the room one last time, wanting to make sure I got everything.

Satisfied, I go back through the hall and meet Sydney, who is standing with her arms wrapped around her own canister.

"All done?" I ask.

She nods.

I follow her out, stepping over the fluid that trails over the back porch and halfway across the driveway. We get to the end of the trail and turn around. I put my canister down, she puts hers beside it.

I take a few more calming breaths, letting months of tension ease out of me. I feel like I could fly. I look down at Sydney. She's been quiet and sullen for the past twenty minutes.

Maybe she's afraid of the legal ramifications, which seems weird to me, considering her normal personality. But, then again, my little sister hasn't been much like herself since I've been home.

I give her the once over, taking in her almost normal clothes and the new pixie cut she's been sporting. Gone are the dreads and the hobo clothes. Gone is the rebel and the unease. Instead, there is a girl who is focused and serious, a girl who takes her meds and goes to her therapy appointments and refuses to talk to me or John about Corey Rossi.

"Got a light?" I ask.

A secret little smile eases into her face. She reaches into her pocket and when she opens her fist, there's a matchbox and a blunt sitting on her palm.

She sticks the blunt in her mouth and begins to light a match.

I scowl at her. "Ugh, really, Syd? You know I hate the smell of—"

She holds up a finger, silencing me as she lights the blunt. She pulls it away from her mouth and blinks up at me. "Have a little faith, would you?" She shoves the box of matches at me. "Here light one."

Frowning, I struggle with the matches. "I hate these things. Don't you have a lighter?"

"I thought matches would be more poetic."

I finally get one lit and hold it out. "Okay!"

She holds her blunt out, matching my pose. "On three."

We count together. "One. Two. Three."

I drop my match. Sydney drops her blunt. They fall in unison, landing on the gasoline so that it blossoms out in a purple *whump* and then races toward the house.

The porch explodes to life and a moment later, the inside of the house follows.

I step close to my little sister and put my arm around her as she does the same. For a moment, we watch, our faces and hearts warmed by the spectacle before us. I tug her closer, bend down and kiss her temple. "I'm proud of you, sis."

Her arm tightens around me and she lays her head on my shoulder. Together, my sister and I watch Cutter's world burn.